MW00875789

IT WAS THE MOST TERRIFYING SCREAM BRITTANY HAD EVER HEARD. . . .

Grant—it was Grant, she was certain—was howling louder than she had ever imagined a person could. Then there was dead silence.

Brittany screwed up her courage and pushed open the door to the boys' locker room. Taking a deep breath, she rushed inside, afraid of what she might see.

Curtis was crouched on the floor, a towel wrapped around his waist, his hair and body dripping wet. He raised his eyes to her in confusion and shock.

On the floor, under Curtis's hand, was Grant Witney. He had on nothing but his shorts and a top. There was an expression of terror, fear, and horror carved into his features. It was as if every muscle in his body had contracted at once, leaving him rigid, his fingers curled into claws.

He was obviously dead.

Books by John Peel

TALONS
SHATTERED
POISON

Available from ARCHWAY Paperbacks

For orders other than by individual consumers, Archway
Books grants a discount on the purchase of **10 or more**
copies of single titles for special markets or premium use.
For further details, please write to the Vice-President of
Special Markets, Pocket Books, 1230 Avenue of the Americas,
New York, NY 10020.

For information on how individual consumers can place
orders, please write to Mail Order Department, Paramount
Publishing, 200 Old Tappan Road, Old Tappan, NJ 07675.

POISON

JOHN PEEL

AN ARCHWAY PAPERBACK
Published by POCKET BOOKS
New York   London   Toronto   Sydney   Tokyo   Singapore

The sale of this book without its cover is unauthorized. If you purchased this book without a cover, you should be aware that it was reported to the publisher as "unsold and destroyed." Neither the author nor the publisher has received payment for the sale of this "stripped book."

This book is a work of fiction. Names, characters, places and incidents are products of the author's imagination or are used fictitiously. Any resemblance to actual events or locales or persons, living or dead, is entirely coincidental.

AN ARCHWAY PAPERBACK *Original*

An Archway Paperback published by
POCKET BOOKS, a division of Simon & Schuster Inc.
1230 Avenue of the Americas, New York, NY 10020

Copyright © 1994 by John Peel

All rights reserved, including the right to reproduce this book or portions thereof in any form whatsoever. For information address Pocket Books, 1230 Avenue of the Americas, New York, NY 10020

ISBN: 0-671-88736-X

First Archway Paperback printing December 1994

10 9 8 7 6 5 4 3 2 1

AN ARCHWAY PAPERBACK and colophon are registered trademarks of Simon & Schuster Inc.

Cover art by Lee MacLeod

Printed in the U.S.A.

IL 7+

This is for Richie Tankersley Cusick—
a delightful new friend—
and for Rick (not forgetting Hannah and Meg!)

CHAPTER

1

"Ee-yew! That is *so* gross!" Kay Johnson shrieked, her voice filled with disgust.

Brittany Harlow glanced up at her friend. "Come on, Kay," she suggested. "Just touch it."

Kay stared at Brittany as if she had completely lost her mind. "Are you crazy?" She shook her head. Her copper-red hair shimmered in the overhead fluorescent light of the classroom, making her head look as if it were aflame. "No way am I touching that slimy, creepy thing."

With all the patience she could muster, Brittany replied, "Kay, this is a snake. It's not slimy. It's a reptile; it's cold-blooded. It doesn't sweat or anything. It's kind of pleasant to touch. Just open your mind for once and try."

Glaring down at the three-and-a-half-foot-long black snake, Kay shuddered. There were thin yellow stripes running along its body, and its tongue kept darting in and out. "I'm definitely not going to touch that thing! It might bite me!"

"It's a *garter snake,*" Brittany said. "It's nonpoisonous. And it doesn't eat anything bigger than a frog or a mouse."

"I don't care." Kay turned her back on the snake in its glass tank. "I'm still not going to touch it. It looks slimy."

Brittany gave in to the smile twitching at the corners of her mouth. "You touch Grant Witney, and *he's* a lot slimier."

"Grant is—" snapped Kay. "Oh, forget it. Grant is absolutely perfect."

"He's a rat," Brittany said, knowing she wouldn't get through. She really liked Kay, but some things about her made Brittany want to scream. She blew the snake a kiss. "If you were bigger, you'd eat him up, wouldn't you? You'd love to crunch a little rat, huh?"

"You're just jealous," Kay replied meanly. "And it's no wonder you don't have a boyfriend—your idea of a good time is snuggling up to a tarantula or something."

Those words cut into Brittany's good mood. Without saying anything more, she replaced the lid of the glass vivarium.

Realizing she'd hurt her friend, Kay reached out and touched Brittany's arm. "I'm sorry, Brit. That was horrible of me, wasn't it?"

Brittany shrugged. "No, you're right. I do put guys off." She ran a hand through her long dark curls and sighed.

"They just don't appreciate you," Kay said. "You know why? Because you're a lot smarter than they are, and that scares them. You're almost as brilliant as I am beautiful."

"But that difference makes them flock around you and leave me alone," Brittany answered. "The only time they even speak to me is when they want to cheat on exams." She took her glasses off and idly polished them on a tissue. Without them she saw the room as a series of colored blurs. "Guys don't go for girls who wear glasses." She replaced them again, and everything returned to normal.

"Garbage," Kay said. "You just lack self-confidence."

"I think you took my share along with yours."

That made Kay grin. "Probably," she admitted. "'Don't hate me because I'm beautiful,'" she said, quoting her favorite shampoo commercial, and then she laughed. "Anyway, all you need is to believe in yourself." She glanced down at the vivarium. "And stop playing with snakes. That *definitely* turns guys off. Trust me."

Brittany couldn't help smiling. She looked around

the biology lab at the tanks containing her mother's snakes. "I couldn't give them up," she said. "After all, they're my mom's job." Her mother—Dr. Susan Harlow—was the head of ophiology at the nearby zoo, and she had brought the snakes to school for a demonstration in biology classes.

"Then she should keep her job to herself," Kay said firmly. "Look, how much longer do we have to sit here and watch these little creeps anyway? We've already missed the early bus home."

"Not long," Brittany promised. "Mom and Christina should be back any minute. You want to help us load these guys into the van?"

"Moi?" Kay raised her eyebrows in disgust. "You have to be joking. That would be *work,* and I won't even touch the tanks those things live in. I'll just have to try to be happy watching the three of you."

"You're all heart."

Kay grinned wickedly. "Not according to Grant. He says I'm all legs and—" Before she could finish, the door opened, and Dr. Harlow and her assistant walked in.

"Sorry to keep you girls waiting," Dr. Harlow apologized. "School paperwork seems to take forever."

"That's okay, Mom," Brittany replied. "You want a hand out to the van with these tanks?"

Dr. Harlow looked at Kay. "Are you volunteering, too? It doesn't sound like you."

Kay held up her hands. "I never said a word. I'll just watch."

Christina Ash frowned slightly. She was Dr. Harlow's assistant, but where the doctor was tall, with long dark hair—just turning gray—Christina was petite and fair. Her short blond hair framed her thin face like a cap, and gave her an elfin appearance. Her hair, coupled with her pale, watery blue eyes, made her appear both otherworldly and attractive.

"What's wrong?" she asked, her voice lightly accented. "Scared of hard work?"

"No," Kay answered. "Allergic. It makes me break out in cold sweats and ruins my good looks."

Brittany stepped in. This was the first time Christina had met Kay, and Kay could be a little hard to take. "She's terrified of snakes," she explained. Brittany knew that was why Kay was making a joke out of this—to cover up her fear.

"Oh." Christina acted as if she'd never considered it possible that anyone might be scared of snakes. "Well, would you mind holding the doors open for us, at least?"

"Sure," Kay agreed. As the others each picked up a vivarium, Kay opened the door to the empty hallway. After they were through, she closed it and ran past them to open the door to the parking lot. A sunny early-spring day in suburban Chicago greeted them.

The back doors of the zoo van were open and the transport shelves cleared for the tanks. The tanks would be fastened in place for the drive back to the zoo. The transfer of the tanks went smoothly, and they all headed back to the biology lab for more tanks.

As they reentered the school, Brittany noticed that

there were a few other kids in the hall now. She stiffened in shock when she noticed two of them locked in a pretty passionate embrace at the end of the hall. The girl's frizzy blond hair and short skirt made her instantly identifiable as Donna Bryce, the class tramp.

Even with his back to them, the guy with her could only be one person.

"Grant!" Kay howled furiously and took off down the hall.

"Uh-oh," muttered Brittany. She cast an apologetic look at her mother, then raced after her friend.

Grant Witney twisted around, still locked in Donna's viselike grip. He had smudged lipstick over one ear and half of his neck. His handsome face was marred by a frown as he saw Kay hurtling toward him. "Oh. Hi, Kay."

Grinding to a halt just two feet from him, Kay's face was almost as red as her hair. "Is that all you've got to say?" she yelled.

Not at all upset, Grant just shrugged. "Yeah. I'm kind of busy right now," he said.

"Yeah—trading spit with *her*," Kay snarled. She glowered at Donna, who just licked her lips and then stuck out her tongue. Kay was on the verge of either screaming or punching someone. Brittany knew her friend had a temper at the best of times, and this was hardly the best of any time.

"Hey, relax," Grant said. "There's plenty of me to go around, babe. I'll get to you later, I promise."

Kay was livid. "The hell you will," she snapped.

"Nobody disses me like this, Witney. We're through."
She was gritting her teeth hard, apparently to keep
from sinking them into his arm.

Grant shrugged. "Suit yourself," he said, uncon-
cerned. "It's your loss."

Brittany grabbed her friend's arm. "Kay," she said
quietly and urgently. "Don't let him get to you."

"Get to me?" Kay shook her head. "I won't let him
get to me. I'll just *murder* the rat!" With a howl she
whipped her fist around in an arc and slammed it into
his stomach.

Grant was an athlete, with a tight, strong body. But
he hadn't been expecting that punch. His breath
whooshed out and he turned almost purple as he
collapsed to the floor, dragging Donna down in a
squealing heap.

"Get up, you toad!" Kay yelled at him. She was
rubbing her wrist, clearly in pain from the punch
she'd struck. "I'm gonna knock you down again!"

Pushing Donna away, Grant sprang to his feet,
wheezing slightly. He bunched up his own fist, his face
twisted with anger and humiliation. He seemed to be
all set to punch Kay out in return, but another boy ran
up and grabbed his wrist. Brittany saw it was her
cousin, Curtis.

"Don't do it, Grant," Curtis said. "Let it go."

"Nobody hits me and gets away with it," Grant
growled, trying without success to shake Curtis off.

"She's a girl," Curtis reminded him.

"And I'm gonna beat the crap out of him!" Kay
yelled. Brittany tried to drag her back, but Kay was

too angry to be restrained. "Come on, toad-spit. Just *try* me!"

Grant shook his head. "It wouldn't be a fair fight," he said, managing to control his temper. "I'm outta here."

"You're dead meat!" Kay screamed. "I'm gonna get you for this, Witney!" He ignored her and walked off with Curtis.

The other students who had gathered seemed embarrassed and uncertain about what to do. Brittany knew that the news of this would spread around school the next day in minutes. She felt terrible for Kay. She'd tried to warn her friend what Grant was like, but Kay was never very good at listening to advice. Catching him like this was probably the only way she'd believe what a jerk he was. But it hurt Brittany to see her friend humiliated.

Donna had managed to get up. She was glaring spitefully at Kay. "He doesn't need you," she said frostily. "He's got me now. If you'd been half the girl I am, he wouldn't have needed me. I'm all he can handle."

"Oh, yeah?" said Kay in a quiet and deadly voice. "Then handle this, you tramp." She whipped her hand around and slapped Donna's cheek. With a yowl of pain, Donna collapsed on the floor again, whimpering. Kay spun around and stomped off.

Brittany couldn't resist humiliating Donna further. "Pull your skirt down, Donna," she said, her voice dripping with sweetness. "The boys can see everything you've got. Oh, but I forgot—they've seen it all before, haven't they?"

She caught up with her friend and said: "Kay—"

Kay was breathing heavily and refused to meet Brittany's gaze. "That filthy little creep," she muttered coldly. Brushing past Dr. Harlow and Christina —who both looked shocked—she reentered the biology lab, Brittany close on her heels. Wrenching the lid off the closest tank, Kay reached in and picked up a snake and then turned to Brittany.

"You're right," she said coldly. "It *is* better than touching Witney." She glanced down at the snake. "Is this poisonous?"

"No," Brittany said hastily. "You're okay. Mom doesn't bring any venomous snakes to schools."

"Pity," Kay said as she replaced it. "I really could have used it if it was. On Witney." Shaking her head, she snapped, "Haven't we got work to do?"

Brittany just stared at her in amazement. Kay *must* be in shock!

CHAPTER

2

Kay marched past Dr. Harlow and Christina, carrying a tank, ignoring both of them completely. Brittany, struggling through the door with a second tank, found herself confronting two puzzled and angry faces.

"Does your friend always behave like this?" asked Christina. "She is so undisciplined and aggressive! I had thought you'd choose your friends a little more carefully, Brittany."

Brittany felt herself turning red. "That's not fair," she snapped, defending Kay. "She's not normally like this." Honesty compelled her to add, "Well, not *that* aggressive."

Dr. Harlow shook her head. "Brittany, I wish you'd distance yourself from Kay. She's going to get herself into trouble, you mark my words."

Stung, Brittany replied: "You both must have seen what happened. It wasn't her fault. She was provoked."

"That's no excuse for acting like a barbarian and using physical force," Christina retorted.

"What is an excuse?" asked Kay from the doorway. "Hearing someone talk about you behind your back?" She glared at Christina. "Keep your nose out of this—it's none of your business. Do you want my help or not?"

"Please," begged Brittany, "don't fight." It was increasingly obvious that Kay and Christina had taken an instant dislike to each other. Brittany liked both girls and knew she was going to end up in the middle.

"No, we don't want your help," said Christina firmly, answering Kay's question.

"Fine!" Kay shouted. "I'd rather be alone, anyway." Setting the tank she held down on the floor, she took off.

"Kay, wait!" called Brittany.

"I said I wanted to be alone!" she called back without turning around. Tossing her long copper hair so that it blazed in the light, Kay indicated she was finished talking. Seconds later she vanished down another corridor.

Brittany felt her mother's hand on her shoulder, giving it a gentle squeeze. "I know you feel bad for her," Dr. Harlow said. "But she's probably better off on her own right now. She must have a lot of poison in her system."

"She's a brat," muttered Christina, clearly still annoyed.

"No, she isn't," Brittany said in defense of her friend. "She's hurting, that's all." Aware of the tank she was still holding, she added: "Maybe we should get this finished before my arms drop off?"

With the three of them working, it didn't take long to get the van loaded again. Christina fastened the tanks in place, and Dr. Harlow gave her daughter a thin smile.

"I've got to take these back to the zoo, love," she said, glancing at her watch. "I should be home around six, I think. Will you be fine till then?"

"Sure," Brittany replied. "I'll take the late bus home in about half an hour."

"Would you rather have a ride?" Christina asked from inside the van. "I came in my car, and I could drop you off on my way home." She hopped out. "Your mother gave me time off. I've got what I think you Americans call a hot date tonight."

"Thanks, but not today," Brittany answered. She sighed. "I'll just hang around awhile, in case Kay decides she wants to talk after all." She managed a smile. "Have fun."

"I *always* have fun," Christina told her.

"I'm glad one of us does," muttered Brittany. She

waved to both of them and then slowly walked back into school. She really didn't have any place to go, as classes were over for the day. The only kids left were the ones with after-school activities.

She felt really bad for Kay—Grant Witney was *such* a jerk, humiliating her like that in public. On the other hand, she'd tried to warn Kay what the guy was like, but Kay refused to listen. Then again, what right did *she* have, giving Kay advice on boys? Guys always buzzed around Kay. She might be down now, but she'd find a new guy soon and be back to her usual cheery self. She wouldn't let a jerk like Witney keep her down.

Brittany caught a glimpse of her reflection in a display case as she passed it and sighed. The only guys who ever asked her out were ones who wanted to get closer to Kay by dating her best friend. *Face it,* she told herself, *you're no great beauty.*

When she was depressed, Brittany thought that Kay only hung out with her so that she'd shine even more. That often happened—a pretty girl would hang around with plainer ones so she'd be the one the guys stared at. But Brittany knew it wasn't really true with Kay. For one thing, Kay stood out in anyone's company. With her copper curls and body to die for, she had no need of a geeky friend to be compared against. Also, Kay was basically too decent to treat Brittany that way. For all her moodiness and that temper of hers, Kay was a really nice and kind person, and Brittany enjoyed her company.

Then why did she do something dumb like punching out Grant and Donna?

As if on cue, Donna Bryce came storming around the next corner, almost flattening Brittany in the process. There was a livid red blotch on her cheek where Kay had slapped her. The rest of her face turned almost the same color when she recognized Brittany.

"You'd better keep Kay Johnson out of my way," she snarled, stabbing a finger at Brittany. "Because when I find her, I'm going to kill her."

"Oh, calm down, Donna," Brittany replied. "I know she slapped you, but you asked for it. You *did* steal her boyfriend, even if it was just that pig Witney." Unable to resist twisting the knife, she added, "And the swelling will go down in a week or so, I'm sure."

"I don't mean I'd kill her for the slap," Donna snapped. "But because Grant just *dumped* me."

"Really?" Brittany said with mock sympathy. "Gee, what a shame. I guess you must be losing your sex appeal."

"It's all that Johnson witch's fault," Donna pressed on. "She drove him to do it. He was so freaked out by her."

"Let's face it, Donna," said Brittany, "you've been dumped more times than a trash can."

"It was never by *Grant Witney* before! And after all I've done for him, too!"

Brittany rolled her eyes. She could just imagine what Donna had done for Grant. The girl was actually

14

quite a fair athlete, especially in gymnastics. She could twist herself into some pretty bizarre shapes. Being the kind of girl she was, though, Donna tended to use her skills outside the gym.

"I'm going to fix both of them," Donna promised angrily. "They'll learn not to mess with me."

Brittany sighed. "You've been studying clichés again, haven't you? You'll be saying something like 'This town ain't big enough for the both of us' next."

The blond girl glowered at Brittany. "Mock me all you want," she said coldly, with the edge of a threat in her voice.

"Thanks," said Brittany. "I will."

With a grunt, Donna stormed away. Brittany shook her head, bewildered. Things were really happening today! Poor Kay learning the truth about Grant, and then Grant dumping Donna immediately afterward. Well, he probably had another girl or six lined up to take their places. So far, he'd managed to anger only about a quarter of the girls in school; he was obviously going for a much higher percentage.

Brittany didn't know exactly why she decided to hang around. Maybe in case Kay needed to talk, but she had no real idea where Kay might be.

She knew where Grant was. In the gym. He was on the weight-lifting team, along with Brittany's cousin Curtis, though Grant was far superior. His well-developed pecs were his main appeal for the opposite sex. Brittany had never thought of bulging muscles as sexy, but there were plenty of girls who did.

She was struck right then by the thought that Donna

had been heading in the direction of the gym when she'd run into her. Had she gone there to catch up with Grant? If so, there might be another interesting scene. Brittany struggled briefly with her conscience, knowing that it was none of her business what went on between that pair. As she'd expected, her conscience lost. No way was she going to miss out witnessing what might be the fight of the decade.

She hurried along the practically deserted corridors toward the locker rooms and gym. As she drew closer to them, she suddenly slowed her pace. The weirdest feeling had come over her.

The hairs on the back of her neck were rising. She felt goose bumps springing up all over her body, as her skin grew cold and clammy. A ringing sound in her ears added to the creepy sensation that she was being watched.

She'd never felt anything like it before. It was as if some person were focusing in on her while sending out waves of emotion. Shaken, Brittany spun around. The corridor behind her was empty. Still, she felt eyes on her. Her skin was chilled and she was having difficulty swallowing. Was she sick? Coming down with the flu or something?

A wave of nausea passed over her, and she staggered, as if someone had punched her in the stomach. Gasping for breath, she reeled backward and leaned against the wall for support. What was happening to her? The dreadful certainty that there were malevolent eyes on her refused to go away.

And then it was gone. Slowly Brittany began to recover. Still leaning against the wall, she forced herself to breathe deeply and slowly until she regained her strength and could straighten up.

What happened to me? she asked herself, scared of the answer. Had it been some kind of heart murmur or something? As far as she knew, there was no history of heart disease in her family. But *something* had struck her. What?

As she struggled to find some kind of answer to the question, she was shaken once again. She could hear a loud voice, angry and threatening, coming from the boys' locker room. It sounded like Grant Witney yelling at someone. Well, that wasn't surprising; he had a temper and things hadn't gone too well for him today. He was probably taking his anger out on some poor jerk who was stuck in there.

Then the incoherent words broke off and there was a slamming sound, like something hitting a locker.

The most terrifying scream that Brittany had ever heard followed.

Grant—it was Grant, she was certain—was howling in terror, louder than she had ever imagined a person could.

Then there was dead silence.

Brittany's heart was pounding crazily in her chest. *What had happened?* Grant had been screaming in terror, then—nothing. Did he need help? Scared and worried, Brittany hesitated. Should she get one of the coaches? Or what? She had moved closer and was just outside the locker room now, still uncertain what she should do. Surely there was someone in there with Grant? She'd heard him arguing with someone.

Had that other person done something to Grant?

Knowing she might regret it later, Brittany screwed up her courage and pushed open the door to the boys' locker room. Taking a deep breath, she rushed inside, afraid of what she might see.

Curtis was crouched on the floor, a towel wrapped around his waist, his hair and body dripping wet. He raised his eyes to her in confusion and shock.

On the floor, under Curtis's hand, was Grant Witney. He had on nothing but his shorts and a top. There was an expression of terror, fear, and horror carved into his features. It was as if every muscle in his body had contracted at once, leaving him rigid, his fingers curled into claws.

He was obviously dead; nobody could look like that alive.

Brittany wanted to be sick, but she fought to stay in control. "What . . . ?" she gasped.

Curtis leaped up from the body as if he'd been electrified. "I was in the shower," he gasped. "I heard him scream. I didn't do it!"

"Do it?" repeated Brittany dully. *What was he talking about?*

Then she saw what Curtis had been looking at. On Grant's neck were two punctures, deep into the jugular vein. Blood had dripped down his neck and formed into a large red puddle that continued to spread out from his head. . . .

CHAPTER
3

Brittany felt a rushing sensation as if she were falling into a huge funnel. She knew that she was in danger of fainting. Refusing to succumb, she took a deep breath and then steeled herself to stare at the body again. *Something or someone had bitten Grant on the neck. . . .*

The marks were just like those left by Dracula in old horror movies.

A *vampire?* Brittany couldn't believe it.

"It wasn't me," Curtis repeated. His voice sounded

thin and whiny, and Brittany realized he was as shaken as she was. "I was in the shower and I heard him scream. I ran in and . . ." He gestured at the body. "There he was."

It didn't make any sense. Brittany shook her head, then wished she hadn't as a wave of giddiness swept over her. "I heard him arguing with somebody," she said. They were the only two living people in the locker room.

"There—there wasn't anybody here when I came out of the shower," Curtis said, confused. "And *you* were the first person to come in."

Brittany couldn't understand it. There were only two doors in or out of the locker room: the main door and the door to the showers. There was no door leading directly into the gym itself. Neither Curtis nor Brittany saw anybody, and Brittany didn't want to know where that thought led! Instead, she glanced down at Grant's body again. Forcing herself to think, she said, "You'd better get dressed. I'll go find the weight-lifting coach. He'll have to call the police, I guess."

"Police?" Curtis almost jumped at the word.

"Of course," she told him. "Curtis, Grant's *dead*. The police have to be called." What was he so worried about? Unless—

Unless he was lying about being in the shower. Or about not having seen anyone. Was he covering up for someone who had done this? Or—

Had *he* killed Grant?

Shaking, Brittany spun around and almost threw herself out the door. She was glad to be away from Grant's body. She'd never seen anyone dead before, except her grandfather at his wake, and that was different. She'd been prepared for him to be laid out in a coffin.

Nothing could have prepared her for what she had just seen.

"Hey!"

Brittany was startled to see the coach heading toward her down the short corridor from the gym.

"What the devil were you doing?" he yelled. "I saw you come out of there! What were you up to in the boys' locker room?"

Brittany stammered: "I—I . . ." She swallowed hard. "Grant Witney's in there," she said.

"So you're another of his girlfriends?" the coach demanded angrily. "That's no excuse for being in the boys' locker room."

"Listen to me!" Brittany screamed, amazed at the panic in her voice. She must be closer to losing it than she realized. "He's *dead!* I heard him scream. I went in to check!"

That stopped the coach in his tracks. "Dead?" he repeated, pushing her aside to rush into the locker room. Brittany started to follow, but couldn't.

She couldn't look at the body again.

"Brittany!"

Brittany saw with relief that it was Kay, hurrying toward her. "Kay! Thank goodness!"

"What's wrong?" Kay asked, concerned. "You're as white as milk!" She put out an arm to steady her friend.

"It's Grant," Brittany said, trying to regain her composure.

"Grant?" Kay clearly didn't understand her, then her face went red. "If he did anything to you, I'll kill him!"

Brittany was warmed by her friend's support, and chilled by her choice of words. "You're too late for that," she said quietly. "Somebody's beaten you to it."

"What?" Kay stared at her, puzzled. "What are you talking about? Are you joking?"

"I wish," muttered Brittany. "He's *dead.*"

Kay reacted as if she'd been punched in the stomach. The color drained from her face. She struggled to speak, but nothing came out.

The door across the corridor suddenly swung open. Brittany saw Donna Bryce standing in the doorway to the girls' locker room. She was dressed in a leotard, with a towel slung around her neck. She appeared tired, but oddly pleased.

"Did I hear you right, Harlow?" she asked. "Grant's dead?"

Brittany nodded, holding up Kay, who looked as if she might faint any moment.

Donna nodded. "Good." She started to go back into the locker room.

"Good?" echoed Brittany, aghast. "How can you say that? He's *dead!*"

"He deserved it," Donna said, her voice curiously even and controlled. Without another word she stepped into the locker room, the door swinging closed behind her.

Brittany's head was whirling. What was happening to everyone? Grant was dead; Kay was in a state of shock; Donna was acting as if nothing was wrong; and Curtis had behaved as if Brittany had accused him of killing Grant. Brittany felt like screaming.

The door to the boys' locker room swung out, and the coach—she couldn't remember his name—came out. He looked sick, his face pale and beaded with sweat. "Don't let anyone in there," he gasped to her. "I'm calling the police."

Brittany managed to nod, still supporting Kay. The coach rushed to his office and slammed the door behind him. The noise jerked Kay back to life.

"What happened to him?" she demanded, obviously meaning Grant.

"I don't know," Brittany admitted. "But it must have been very painful. He died in agony, that much was obvious."

"Was it . . ." Kay began. Then she had to take a deep breath and start again. "Was it natural? Some kind of sickness?"

It was the question that Brittany had been deliberately avoiding. "No," she finally answered, her voice low and thin. "I think he was murdered."

A short while later the locker room area was a mass of confusion. Brittany couldn't believe how many people had arrived. An ambulance with medics came, even though there was nothing to be done for Grant. At least four police cruisers had pulled up outside, and several uniformed officers cordoned off the end of the building with their strips of yellow tape strung between poles. A couple others took initial statements from everyone, and two more officers were on guard outside the door to the boys' locker room. Everyone who had been in or around the gymnasium at the time of the death had been assembled in one large classroom and told not to talk to one another until they had been questioned.

Brittany sat in shocked silence, waiting in the classroom. She was biting at her lower lip, her stomach churning. Her right hand was being gripped ferociously by Kay's left. With the fingers of her other hand, Kay was twining and untwining her hair, over and over. Her eyes were wide and she looked terribly shocked, as if she was barely holding on to her sanity.

Donna Bryce sat at the back of the room, dressed in street clothes again. She was leaning her head against the back wall, her feet up on a second chair. She appeared to be quite relaxed. Curtis was seated by the windows, staring out at the people milling around in the parking lot. His hands were shaking, and he appeared pale. There were a few other students, boys who had been working out in the gym. Brittany didn't know their names. They appeared confused and a little annoyed.

The coach was seated behind the desk, carefully not

looking at Miss Yates, the girls' P.E. teacher. She appeared strained and nervous and was picking at her nail polish. Brittany realized she must have been in her office or in the other locker room at the time of Grant's death. So why hadn't she come out when he screamed?

The last person in the room was a police officer, standing guard beside the door. She never spoke, nor looked at them. But it was obvious she was there to observe them as well as to prevent them from talking to one another.

Brittany knew the police didn't want any of them exchanging details or fabricating alibis. That meant the police obviously thought Grant's death was murder.

Were they all suspects? Brittany didn't know, which didn't help the gnawing pangs in her stomach. Part of them were from hunger—she was way late for dinner —but most of them were from nerves. She wondered if anyone had thought to call her mother to tell her where she was. Or was her mom home now, worrying and trying to find her?

The door opened, and two more people walked in. Both were in civilian clothing, but had *police* written all over them. One was a middle-aged man, heavyset with his stomach bulging over the top of his belt. He looked tired and grizzled. The other was a slim young woman with piercing eyes and a slightly quizzical expression. Her dark hair was cropped almost as short as her companion's. She was the one who spoke.

"I'm Detective Sergeant Kahn," she said. Her voice was firm and strong. "This is Detective Sergeant Jellicoe. I'm sorry that you've all been kept here so late, but we have to ask each of you a few questions. Then you'll be allowed to go home."

Donna came back to life at this. "Aren't we supposed to call our lawyers or something?"

Sergeant Kahn smiled slightly. "That's only if you're suspected of a crime. Right now you're simply witnesses. We just want to find out what happened."

Miss Yates half raised her hand, then stopped sheepishly. "Uh, I'm not a witness. I was—"

"Even that can be important in an investigation of this kind," Kahn broke in quickly. "Please, just wait till we talk to you. Now, are there any more questions before we start?"

It sounded like a school math test! Brittany cleared her throat. "Has anyone called my mother? She'll be wondering where I am."

Sergeant Kahn glanced across at the uniformed officer who'd been watching them. The woman gave a slight shake of her head. "Good point," the detective agreed. "Perhaps you'd better all write down the name and number of someone we can contact about where you are. Give it to the officer here, and we'll make certain your relatives are notified and reassured." She glanced at her companion.

Sergeant Jellicoe studied a small notepad in his hand. "Curtis Harlow."

Curtis jumped to his feet, flushing.

"Come along with us, please," Jellicoe requested. "The rest of you, please just wait your turns. We'll get to you all as quickly as we can." Curtis—looking as if he were being taken to face a firing squad—was led from the room.

Brittany gave Kay a wan smile and squeezed her hand. Kay didn't respond and seemed totally out of it, which worried Brittany. Usually her friend was so fiercely independent, but she was so clingy now. She knew that even though Kay had broken up with Grant earlier, it would be impossible just to switch off her emotions when she discovered he was dead.

The uniformed officer went around the room with a notepad for them all to scribble down the phone number and name of someone to contact. Kay clearly had to force herself to focus long enough to jot down her parents' number. As soon as she had, she lapsed back into her thoughts, clutching hard at Brittany's hand.

It was only minutes before beefy Sergeant Jellicoe appeared at the door and called Brittany's name. She stood up and had to pry herself free of Kay's grip. It was hard to tell if Kay noticed the nod and smile Brittany gave her. Swallowing nervously, Brittany then followed Jellicoe to another classroom. It felt more and more as if she were facing a test of some kind.

Sergeant Kahn was seated at the teacher's desk. In front of her was a tape recorder and a notepad. She gave Brittany a reassuring smile and gestured for her to sit beside the desk. As Brittany sat she tried to gather her emotions. She heard Jellicoe take a seat in a row behind her somewhere.

Sergeant Kahn studied her pad. "Brittany Harlow, right?" When Brittany nodded, she asked: "Are you related to Curtis Harlow?"

"We're cousins," Brittany explained. She noticed that the tape recorder was already in motion. They were taking no chance of missing anything!

"And could you tell us how you came to see Grant Witney?"

Nervously Brittany explained everything. Sergeant Kahn nodded and smiled, but said little until Brittany was finished. Then she pounced.

"Why did you go to the locker area?"

Shrugging, Brittany said, "I'm not sure. I was half looking for Kay, and half . . ." She sighed. "I kind of figured that Donna might have another fight with Grant, and I was kind of curious."

"You didn't enter the locker room right away when you heard the scream?"

"No. I hesitated for . . . I guess about fifteen seconds or so."

Kahn frowned. "Why?"

"It was the *boys'* locker room."

"I see." The detective paused a moment. "And there was no one with you in the corridor?"

"No."

"Did anyone see you as you went to the locker room?"

Brittany thought back. "I don't think so. It was

pretty deserted." She wondered what the point of the questions was.

"And nobody came out of the boys' locker room before you went in?"

"No."

Kahn nodded. "Yet you heard Grant arguing with someone inside?"

"Yes." Brittany felt more nervous suddenly. "I didn't hear who the other person was, but Grant sounded very angry."

"And when you did go in, you saw Curtis Harlow bent over the body?"

Brittany nodded. The sergeant gestured at the tape recorder, and Brittany realized she had to speak. "Oh, yes, that's right."

"He was wet and dressed only in a towel?"

"Yes. He said he'd been taking a shower and came out when he heard Grant scream."

"Did you hear the shower going when you were in the locker room?" Sergeant Kahn leaned forward, her eyes narrowing.

Trying to think back, Brittany could only shrug. "I don't know. I wasn't listening. I don't think so. I'm not sure."

Kahn nodded. "So Curtis heard the scream, turned off the shower, wrapped on a towel, and went into the other room to the body. All in, you say, about fifteen seconds?"

"I guess . . ." Brittany realized all at once what the woman was getting at. "You think *Curtis* killed Grant?"

"I don't *think* anything yet," Kahn replied. "I'm just studying the subject, so to speak. There was nobody else in the locker room, and the only two doors were the one you entered by and the one Curtis entered by?"

Wondering if she'd just landed her cousin in trouble, Brittany shook her head. "Nobody. And there's no other way into the locker room."

"There's one small window," put in Sergeant Jellicoe from behind her. "Was it open?"

"Window?" Brittany concentrated. She'd never been in the boys' room before, and she had to think hard. She had seen a small window. "Oh, yes, I do remember it. But it's very small. I don't recall if it was open. I wasn't really looking at it," she said apologetically. "Nobody could have climbed through it, surely?"

Sergeant Kahn shrugged. "Not unless he was a contortionist, no."

Contortionist? Brittany gave a start. "Donna's double-jointed!" But could even she have slipped through such a tiny window? She didn't know.

The dark woman raised an eyebrow. "That would be Donna Bryce, Grant's girlfriend?"

"Ex-girlfriend. He'd just sent her packing," Brittany explained.

"And you saw her come out of the girls' locker room a few minutes later?"

"That's right," Brittany agreed. "She looked tired and seemed happy to hear Grant was dead."

"I see." Kahn frowned. "And this other friend of yours"—she studied her pad—"Kay Johnson. According to Curtis, she had been dating Grant and had punched him—and slapped Donna—earlier. At that time she threatened to kill him. Is that right?"

"Kay?" said Brittany, aghast. "You think *Kay* did it?"

The sergeant sighed. "I told you, I don't think *anything* yet. I'm just trying to get at the facts. Now, please, answer the question: Did Kay threaten to kill Grant?"

"Well, yes," agreed Brittany, feeling like a traitor. "But she was angry. She has a bit of a temper, and she was just reacting out of anger."

"She has a bad temper?" Kahn asked, significantly.

"I didn't mean it like that!" insisted Brittany. "She says things, but she's not violent."

"Really?" asked Jellicoe lazily. "She punches Grant, floors Donna, and then threatens to kill Grant, who turns up dead. And you don't think she's *violent?"*

"You're twisting my words," Brittany protested. She felt terrible, making Kay look like a suspect instead of supporting her. "And she wasn't anywhere near the locker room anyway."

"She must have been," Kahn pointed out. "You told us that she came up to you just after the death."

Brittany felt confused. "I mean . . . well, she came from down the hall."

"I see." The detective studied Brittany carefully.

"Just a couple more questions. You didn't go into the locker room till *after* Grant screamed? Not *before?*"

"Before?" Brittany was totally bewildered now. "No. Why would I have gone in before?"

"Why indeed?" Sergeant Kahn studied her pad again. "According to Curtis, it was about thirty seconds before he got to Grant's body and you came in. Could it have been thirty seconds, not fifteen?"

"I don't know," Brittany admitted. "I was in shock. It might have been, I suppose. I don't know for sure."

"In other words, if you *had* been inside the room— for any reason—there *might* have been time for you to go out again and then reenter the room as if you were going in for the first time?"

It took Brittany several seconds to realize what she was being asked. Then she went red. "You mean was *I* the one who killed Grant?"

"Nobody's accusing you of anything," Jellicoe said smoothly from behind Brittany. "We're just asking if you had time to get out and back in again."

"How would I know!" yelled Brittany. "I didn't do anything! Why would you think I did?"

Sergeant Kahn shook her head. *"We* didn't say you did. Or that we even think you did. We're just asking questions. That'll be all for now, thank you. We may need to call you back in the future. We have your address, and if we need you, we'll be in contact. If you'll just accompany Sergeant Jellicoe now . . ."

Her head in a whirl, Brittany stood up and followed

the beefy sergeant outside. She felt so confused. The police made just about everyone a suspect in the killing of Grant—including her!

Oddly, though, they had not mentioned those strange marks on Grant's throat. . . . She wondered what the police had made of those.

CHAPTER
4

Somehow Brittany made it through the rest of the evening. Her mother was waiting for her when she finally left the school. They stopped for a take-out pizza on the way home, and her mom had insisted on Brittany eating before they talked. Despite her insistence that she couldn't eat anything after all she'd been through, Brittany finished two slices. She had no idea if they were pepperoni, plain, or with everything on them. Then, finally, her mother listened to her story.

"Well, no one could ever accuse you of leading a dull life," her mother said. "Poor thing; how do you feel?"

"Mostly confused," admitted Brittany. "I've got all these emotions bubbling inside me, and there's no telling which one will take over. One minute I feel sorry for Grant; the next, I'm angry that the detective practically accused me of killing him."

"She was just doing her job." Her mom sighed. "They have to consider everyone a suspect. Let's face it, *you* know you didn't do anything, but *they* don't. How's Kay doing? She relies on you so much."

"Kay relies on *me?"* echoed Brittany, unable to believe it. "You've got to be kidding! Kay doesn't need anybody."

Her mother sniffed. "Don't you believe it. *Everybody* needs somebody. Kay leans on you for support more than you know, only she makes it look like she's doing you a favor."

"I think you've got it backward," Brittany told her. "But she *is* having a rough time. It's one thing to find your boyfriend making out with someone else; it's another to find him murdered. She's in shock."

Her mom nodded as she narrowed her eyes. "You don't think Kay *could* have killed Grant, do you?"

"Mom!" Brittany was shocked. "You know Kay better than that! She may scream and yell a lot, but it's just her way of letting off steam. She'd never hurt anyone."

"She punched Grant and this girl Donna."

"That was different," objected Brittany. "She was provoked. *Anyone* would have hit them."

"Would you?"

Brittany forced herself to be honest. "Well, no," she admitted. "But I'm different. I'm a wimp."

"You are not," her mother said. "You've got more sense than to fight in public. And more dignity." She gave her a quirky smile. "Now, that's enough about Grant's death for one evening. Let's watch some mindless TV for a while, shall we? I want you bored enough to go to bed and fall asleep without having nightmares." She zapped the TV with the remote.

Brittany cuddled against her mother, feeling better with her mom's arm round her shoulders. It felt good to be held. She hadn't been this confused, angry, or scared since her father had died. That had been six years earlier; he'd gone off to a conference and never returned. On the way home his plane had crashed. Only six people died, but he'd been one of them. Brittany had had nightmares for two years after that, and even now the thought of getting into a plane made her break out in a cold sweat. She knew it was an irrational fear, but couldn't help it. Some things can't be argued away by logic; gut feelings are too strong for that.

"Mom," she finally said.

"Mmm?"

"Have you ever thought about getting married again?"

Her mother stared down at her. "Why? Do you

want a stepfather, or is this just an attempt to set me up with someone?"

"Seriously!"

Mom shrugged. "Of course I've thought about it. I just haven't ever met anyone I like even a tenth as much as your father, that's all. I haven't ruled out the possibility; a man is just not the most important thing in my life."

"What is?"

"You are." She punched Brittany lightly on the arm. "Then I guess my work; my colleagues; my friends; my snakes." She grinned abruptly. It lit up her face, and Brittany liked the effect. "I remember one time, a couple of years back, Fran at the zoo set me up on a blind date with her cousin. Talk about dull! Anyway, he turned green when I told him I worked with snakes. It seems he was terrified of them. Even more terrified than when he discovered I had a teenage daughter. You scared him silly!" She chuckled. "It's a rare man who could accept both a teenage girl and a bunch of snakes as rivals. I guess that's one reason I've never been serious about another man. That and the fact that I'm very picky. You take after me in that."

"Me?" Brittany laughed. "Right, guys are falling all over themselves to date me. I have to fight them off with sticks."

Her mother eyed her strangely. "I think you just don't notice, Brittany." She smiled again. "Maybe you've got more important things to think about, too."

"I wish."

Eventually they made a joint decision to go to bed. Brittany changed into a nightie and slipped between the sheets of her bed. She felt comforted as she listened to her mother wash up in the bathroom, call good night, and go into her own room.

The problem was, though, that she couldn't get to sleep. Her mind kept turning over the events of the day. It was impossible not to think about them. Eventually she stopped trying to fight her thoughts, and lay on her back, staring at the ceiling, and tried to sort out through them. Her mind turned to the Sherlock Holmes stories she'd read a couple of years before. She liked his method of always following the logical train of thought, no matter where it led.

Fact: Grant Witney was dead. Well, that was a start anyway. Now, there were two possible reasons: He'd died of natural causes, or he'd been killed by someone. Okay, she told herself, try the first reason—natural causes. What natural cause could have killed him instantly and left his muscles contracted and tense? A heart attack? She didn't know. But then there was the fact of his arguing with another person, then that slamming sound, and then his scream.

Then there were those puncture marks on his neck. Where had they come from? Could they have been the cause of his death? Taking all the facts together, she couldn't believe that Grant had died of natural causes.

Which meant that someone had to have killed him. But who? And how?

Back to logic. When she'd gone into the locker

room, she saw Curtis bent over Grant. Curtis had acted strangely. Had it been out of guilt? Or simply because he was afraid that Brittany would think he'd killed Grant? Either way, he claimed to have come in after Grant was dead. Okay, there were only two possibilities: one, he was telling the truth; two, he was lying.

Assume he was telling the truth first. If he *had* found Grant dead, then it explained nothing. He said he'd seen nobody else, and there certainly hadn't been anyone else in the room. So Curtis could have been truthful. Brittany wasn't too sure about that; he was her cousin, all right, but she'd never really liked him. He could be a bit mean and sneaky. He'd done plenty of spiteful things to her when they were younger, and for the past couple of years they'd ignored each other at school and at family gatherings. But that was normal for a jerk his age, right? She honestly didn't think he was capable of killing anyone.

But *somebody* had to have killed Grant, and she had seen Curtis bending over the body. If this was a Perry Mason movie, that would be a sure sign of his innocence—but this was real life, not TV. Maybe he acted guilty because he *was* guilty.

Okay, assume that he's lying. It could be to protect himself or to protect someone else. If he was protecting himself, though, surely he'd come up with a better story? Unless . . .

Maybe *he* had suggested to Sergeant Kahn that Brittany killed Grant. That would have cast suspicion on her and away from himself . . . If he *had* blamed her, she'd make sure that he was caught. But, of course, she didn't know whether he'd blamed her or not.

If he was lying to protect someone else, he *had* seen the killer, and, for some reason, Curtis didn't want him caught. He could have helped the killer to hide in the shower room and then sneaked him out in the confusion later.

Good, except for two things: Curtis hadn't known that Brittany was going to burst in; and *who* would he have covered up for?

She wasn't getting too far. Curtis *could* have been the killer, or else he *could* be covering up for the killer for some reason. If she assumed that Curtis *hadn't* killed Grant, then who did?

Unfortunately, Kay was a prime suspect. Brittany didn't honestly believe that her friend had done it, but Kay did have a motive and had threatened to kill Grant. On the other hand, Kay often shot off her mouth without thinking. She often acted as if her brain had stopped functioning, and this day was definitely one of those times.

Be ruthless, she told herself. *Follow the logic through, even if you don't believe it.* If Kay had been the killer, how could she have escaped and come back without being seen? The only way out that hadn't been watched was one small window near the ceiling. Brittany couldn't imagine Kay slipping through it. She wasn't exactly the world's best athlete. She'd have had to jump onto a bench, pull herself through a tiny window, and then slide down the other side of the wall—and all in about fifteen to thirty seconds. No way.

The other possibility was that Kay could have killed Grant, and then convinced Curtis to cover for her. That made even less sense. She and Curtis had never gotten along. So, thankfully, Brittany was sure that Kay couldn't have been the killer.

Then who else? The other logical suspect was Donna Bryce, who'd just had a fight with Grant and had threatened vengeance. She'd been in the area, and in a leotard. She'd seemed tired when Brittany spoke to her just minutes after the death. Plus, she was extremely athletic. If anyone could have bolted out the window, it was Donna. And if she had been seen by Curtis, she might have convinced him to cover for her. She could certainly have bribed him with the promise of some steamy action later. But would Curtis have accepted sex to cover up for a murder? Brittany didn't really think so—Curtis was much too selfish for that, and he looked out for himself first and always.

It didn't leave many suspects. The coach? But why would he want to kill his star athlete? Miss Yates? Okay, she'd not responded to the scream, but maybe she'd been in the shower and too far away to hear? It was possible. Those other kids from the gym? That was grasping at straws. They would have known Grant, but why would they want to kill him?

Or had there been somebody else? Suspect *X*? Someone who had sneaked in, killed Grant, and then sneaked out without being seen? There wasn't any way to tell. It all depended on how the killer managed to get in and out without being seen.

Then there was the problem of how Grant had been killed so quickly. And what or who had made those marks in his neck. At this point she was *almost* ready to believe that a vampire had flown in the window and bitten him. But it had been in broad daylight, and vampires shriveled up in the sun. Also, vampires were only make-believe. There were no such things.

Or were there?

She realized then that she hadn't told the police or her mother about her weird feeling of being watched and the sudden terror that had overcome her. But surely that had nothing to do with Grant's death. It would only have made her seem more nervous and stupid to the police.

Brittany eventually drifted off to sleep, but it was a sleep filled with a multitude of nightmares. A huge winged serpent took to the air, beating great, impossible wings. The snake then turned into an airplane that crashed into the ground, belching fire and smoke and spilling seats and blood everywhere. Frozen in horror, she could only watch. One of the victims was her father. Another was Grant. As she watched, she was sucked into the still-open jaws of the immense snake and fell, fell, fell . . .

CHAPTER
5

~~~~~

"You look like you slept as well as I did," Brittany said to Kay when she met her friend outside school the following morning. Kay's eyes were puffy and her shoulders were slumped forward.

"Tell me about it," muttered Kay. "I didn't *get* any sleep. I couldn't close my eyes without seeing Grant's dead face."

Brittany frowned. "But you never saw Grant after he was dead."

"In dreams, anything can happen."

"You said you didn't get any sleep," objected Brittany. "So you couldn't have been dreaming."

"What is this?" Kay was almost screaming now. "Are *you* interrogating me? Isn't it bad enough that the cops harassed me for hours? Now *you're* going to start?"

Brittany held up her hands. "Whoa! Kay, I'm sorry. I guess I'm just on edge. I didn't mean to sound like I was cross-examining you."

Swallowing hard, Kay reined in her temper and nodded. "Yeah, I'm sorry, too." She ran her hand through her hair distractedly. "I know I'm being a real grouch." She stopped and stared hard at her friend. "Look, Brit, that detective virtually accused me of killing Grant. It was my own fault, I guess, for what I *did* do yesterday, but I'd appreciate a bit of support from my best friend. Is that too much to ask?"

"Of course it isn't," Brittany replied. She felt her cheeks redden, because she *had* been quizzing Kay. "And if it's any consolation, Sergeant Kahn almost accused me of killing Grant, too. I think she's just letting ideas fly."

"You?" Kay laughed, a harsh, brittle sound, as if she was on the verge of tears. "No offense, Brit, but I can't even imagine you slapping anyone."

"I'm not offended," Brittany said, glancing at the school doors. There seemed to be a lot of people hanging around, and they were all very quiet. "I wonder what's going on?"

Kay blinked as if she was forcing her mind to focus.

"I don't know," she admitted. "But it doesn't look good."

They moved toward the crowd. In the center of it stood Donna Bryce.

"All right, Johnson," she growled at Kay. "Maybe the police weren't smart enough to lock you up for killing Grant, but I'm not going to pretend I don't know the truth."

Brittany could almost hear Kay's blood pressure rising as she took a step forward, her hands balled into fists. The reason for the crowd was obvious now; everyone was expecting a fight between Donna and Kay.

"That's enough," Brittany snapped, moving between them. "The police didn't lock Kay up because she didn't kill Grant."

"We all heard her promise to kill him," Donna snarled. "Are you saying it was just a coincidence that he was dead less than an hour later? What kind of fool do you think I am?"

"Every possible kind," Brittany retorted. "Stop trying to think." She glared at the crowd. "And the rest of you had better remember that we're *innocent until proven guilty.* That goes for Donna as well as Kay and myself."

Donna snorted. "You're claiming that *I* killed Grant? Anything to excuse your pal, is that it?"

"You told me you were going to fix both Grant and Kay," Brittany countered. "Well, Grant's dead, and now you're stirring everyone up against Kay. Come on," she challenged the crowd. "Didn't she ask you to wait here with her till Kay arrived? Didn't she accuse Kay of murder?"

Brian McInnery shuffled his feet uncomfortably as Brittany glared at him. "It *did* seem reasonable," he muttered.

"She's just trying to confuse you all!" Donna cried.

"Right," said Brittany, her voice dripping sarcasm. "And *you're* trying to educate them. A straight D student."

That was a cheap shot, Brittany knew, but it brought a couple of snickers. Donna was at a loss for words, and the other kids started to drift away. Brittany breathed a sigh of relief. She'd acted confident, but she'd been scared silly. To Donna, she said, "Let it be for now. The police are investigating. Give them a chance to accuse someone before you do." Without waiting for a reply, she grabbed Kay's arm and they pushed into the school.

It wasn't a good day. Both Kay and Brittany were completely shunned. It didn't really make them feel better to see that Donna was avoided, too. Kay was thoroughly depressed and demoralized, and Brittany couldn't blame her.

The whole school was under a dark cloud because of Grant's death, of course. Grant had been pretty popular—not for who he was, but because of *what* he was. He'd been a star athlete, a state champion in weight lifting, and ready even for the Olympic trials. The school's hope for fame had been dashed with his death. Curtis was the second best, but hardly in the same league as Grant.

Brittany wondered what her cousin would do as the number one weight lifter in school. Curtis lacked moral and emotional strength. He caved in easily to peer pressure. Brittany knew he'd been drinking at parties, for example. Everyone at school knew they couldn't depend on Curtis.

Which made Brittany's gym class more astonishing than ever.

Brittany *hated* gym. It was an hour of sheer torture for her. It wasn't that she was out of shape or anything; but her eyesight made everything hard for her. She couldn't take gym without her glasses, but wearing them caused other problems. She couldn't judge distances. No captain ever wanted her for her team for any game, which suited Brittany just fine. Spectator was her favorite position in any sport.

Kay, however, was a terrific player, and she'd made it quite clear that anyone who wanted her on a team had better pick Brittany as well. So, despite her best efforts, Brittany was forced to join in because Kay was convinced she was doing Brittany a kindness.

Today in gym nobody wanted either of them, so they got to work out alone on the parallel bars, which Brittany enjoyed. Curtis was the only one in that area of the gym with them, on the bench press, working out, and ignoring everyone.

Kay was, of course, a genius on the bars. She put herself through a routine with ferocious energy, obviously tapping into her anger. Brittany had already worked out enough to sweat and lose her glasses three times. As a result, she wasn't paying too much attention to Kay. Her eyes wandered and focused in on Curtis.

Could *he* have been Grant's killer? He did have opportunity, but did he have some kind of weapon to kill Grant and leave those odd marks in his neck? She almost wished he was guilty, because she never really liked him. And she could almost believe he'd do something stupid to try to get attention.

Curtis was lying out on the bench press, his skin glistening with sweat as he struggled with the weights. His face was contorted into a grimace, and she could make out the tendons and veins in his arms bulging with his effort. Frowning, she stared at the weights he was pressing. There was something not quite right. She couldn't place it at first, but then it came to her, and she stumbled back against the bars.

Kay gave a cry of surprise and lost her grip as the bars shook. She slammed down onto the mat and groaned. "Thanks a lot, Brit."

"Sorry!" Brittany exclaimed. "Are you okay?"

"Oh, yeah," Kay grunted, clambering to her feet. "I just love smashing my wrist. I'm into pain. What on earth did you do that for?"

"I'm sorry," she repeated. Then she remembered what had caused her to stumble. "Kay, look at Curtis."

Her friend glanced at him. "Don't tell me the sight

of your cousin's naked flesh and muscle is turning you on?"

"No, idiot. Look at the *weights.*"

As Kay did so, her eyes widened. "A *hundred and ten* kilos?" she exclaimed.

"He's *never* done better than ninety before," Brittany informed her. "I know—he's complained about it enough."

"And even Grant only managed one-oh-five," Kay added. "We'd better stop Curtis before he—"

They had just started to move when Curtis gave an audible grunt and snatched at the weights. Brittany cut off her warning cry. If she broke his concentration, he could really hurt himself. Besides, there was no way he could—

The weights rose up, shakily, but *up!*

He was doing it!

Then, with a groan, Curtis let them fall back into place, and he lay there, panting and wheezing from the strain.

"Are you trying to kill yourself?" Kay asked him coldly.

It took him a moment to focus on her. "Mind your own . . . business," he said. "I knew . . . I could do it."

"You'll kill yourself," Brittany said unsympathetically.

"No, I won't," he said, swinging his feet down so that he could sit. "I'll be better than Grant ever was. You wait and see." After picking up his towel, he mopped his forehead and moved slowly away.

Brittany turned troubled eyes to her friend. "Did you hear that?" she asked quietly. "Curtis must want to take Grant's place pretty badly. He could have torn his muscles lifting that kind of weight." She finally gave in and asked the question that was burning in her mind. "But did he want Grant's place badly enough to kill him for it?"

Kay scowled. "I don't know. But . . ." She shook her head. "You said that Grant had two puncture marks in his neck. Where?"

"His jugular vein." Brittany held two fingers of her left hand over the faintly pulsing spots on her own neck. "Right here. Why?"

"I guess you didn't notice," Kay said, rubbing her own neck in precisely the same spot. "When Curtis was straining to lift that weight, he had a reddish patch on his neck in that same spot. It almost looked like a hickey."

Brittany frowned. "The same spot? Could it be a coincidence?"

"Could it *be* a hickey?" countered Kay.

"I don't know." Brittany considered the idea. "He goes out now and then with girls, but hardly ever the same one twice."

"Tell me about it." Kay sighed. "I went out with him once."

"You did?" Brittany made barfing motions. "I didn't know you sank that low."

"It taught me a lesson," Kay assured her. "Anyway, to get back to your question. Is it a coincidence? I don't know. But until this murder is solved, I'm going to suspect anything that looks like coincidence."

Taking her time showering, Brittany thought about Curtis. How had he suddenly managed to up his weights by twenty kilos? And what about that mark on his neck? What was it?

Then a suspicion crept into her mind: *You've only got Kay's word that it was there; you didn't see it.* She stuck her head under the tepid stream of water to try to wash away her suspicions. There was no reason to doubt Kay. Was there?

After school she and Kay walked slowly out of the building. The other students hung back to let the two of them leave. Brittany sighed. Oh, well, being under suspicion of murder had one small advantage—they weren't crushed on their way out of school.

Glancing at the parking lot, she stopped. There was her mother's car, with Mom inside it, waving frantically to them. "Kay," she said, nudging her friend and pointing.

Kay glanced up. "Huh? Your mom *never* picks you up unless you're sick."

"I know. Could *this* be a coincidence?" She was relieved to see a small smile appear on Kay's face. "Come on."

They both headed for the car, wondering what was going on.

"Get in," Brittany's mother said urgently. "Quickly!"

They both slid into the backseat of the Eagle Talon. "What's wrong, Dr. Harlow?" Kay asked.

Brittany's mother didn't reply until she had the car in motion. Then she said in a tight voice: "I just wanted to make sure I reached you before the police did."

"The *police?*" Brittany asked, aghast. "What do you mean?"

"I mean," her mother said, casting a worried look in the rearview mirror, "any time now they're going to be hearing some information that will make one or both of you look very much like Grant Witney's killer."

CHAPTER
6

~~~

Brittany heard Kay echo her own gasp. "What are you talking about, Mom?" she begged.

"I want to face you when I tell you," her mother replied evasively. "Be quiet for five minutes, please."

Brittany and Kay exchanged puzzled glances and then tried to stay quiet. It wasn't easy. Brittany was burning with questions, and she knew that Kay was just as eager to find out what was happening. Her mom was behaving as if they were in danger of being arrested any second. Brittany felt worried and scared.

She knew she hadn't done anything, but that was no guarantee somebody else wasn't trying to make her look guilty.

Maybe someone like Curtis?

Dr. Harlow pulled into the parking lot of a small restaurant and led the girls inside and ordered coffee and sodas. When the waitress brought the drinks and then wandered off, Dr. Harlow finally leaned forward to speak.

"I had a call a few hours ago from Dr. Vitelli," she explained. "He works with the local police department as coroner, and he wanted my help to run a serology test, which I thought was odd."

"A what?" asked Kay.

"A blood test," Dr. Harlow explained. "Like you'd get at a hospital. Anyway, as I said, it was odd he'd ask my advice, because I'm not an expert on blood. But I agreed to do it, and he ran some samples over. They were from Grant Witney's body. He'd been conducting the autopsy and run across some really strange readings. As soon as I tried a few simple tests, I could see why. I also knew why he'd come to me.

"Christina and I discovered what killed Grant— snake venom."

"Snake venom?" echoed Brittany, utterly confused. "But . . . how?"

"We'll get to that later," her mother replied grimly. "Anyway, it does explain how Grant died so quickly, and the contractions in his muscles. Both are symptoms of snakebite, if the venom is induced in sufficient quantity. And the level of the toxin in his blood indicated that he'd been given enough venom to kill a herd of horses. I've never found a higher reading in all my years."

"That doesn't make sense," objected Brittany. *"How?"*

"Well, obviously he wasn't bitten by a single snake. Thirty or forty snakes *might* have produced those levels, but there was certainly no chance that this had occurred. Christina and I went with Dr. Vitelli to examine the body, and it was clear what had happened. There was severe toxic shock in Grant's neck area, and his heart had been stopped by the actions of the venom. The venom had definitely been administered in a single dose through those two puncture wounds in his neck." She could see Brittany poised to ask another question and held her hand up. "Let me finish before you interrupt again. Thank you. The indications of death helped us to identify the exact toxin—it was venom from the long-nosed viper. That's a snake native to southern Europe and Asia Minor, not the United States. There are none at all, outside of zoos. We have eight of them. Even if he'd been bitten by all eight at one time, they couldn't have caused those toxin levels in his blood. And he had no snakebites anywhere on his body.

"There is only one possible conclusion: Someone *deliberately* injected Grant with a highly lethal dose of viper venom. Someone who didn't know how much would kill, and therefore gave him a massive amount.

Someone who had access to snake venom." She stared at Brittany and Kay. "Someone like the two of you, in fact."

"What?" Brittany couldn't believe what her mother was saying. She felt betrayed. "You think one of us killed Grant?"

"I didn't say that," Dr. Harlow replied angrily. "I said that you had access to the venom. Both of you come out to see me at the zoo pretty often. We keep the supplies of snake venom in a small refrigerator in my lab. Christina went back to check on the contents, and she called me to say that our entire supply of viper venom is missing. You two were out just three days ago, and the last time the venom was checked was a week ago."

"That's still no reason to accuse us!" snapped Kay.

"I'm not accusing you," Dr. Harlow said. "I know neither of you would have killed Grant. But the *police* are bound to link the venom to you. I wanted to let you know before they did. I think we should go down to the precinct and talk to those two detectives, don't you? They're going to want to talk to you anyway, and it'll look better if you volunteer to help."

"Instead of being arrested?" Kay asked bitterly. "Maybe we can save them the trouble of hunting for us. This way they can just usher us into a nice warm cell."

Dr. Harlow glared at her. "Kay, I'm trying to make allowances for the shock you've been through, but you're starting to irritate me. They won't arrest you— just question you."

Kay sighed and took a long, slow breath. "I'm sorry," she said. "But speaking of questions, I have a couple. What do you keep snake venom for? Isn't that asking for trouble?"

"Quite the opposite," Brittany's mother replied. "We need the venom to make antivenin. If someone is bitten by a snake, he or she has to be treated as quickly as possible. The antivenin must be fresh, so we always keep a supply of venom on hand."

"Oh." Kay looked puzzled. "But I didn't even know you kept the stuff, so how could I have stolen it?"

"I don't think you did," repeated Dr. Harlow. "But the police will."

"Wait a minute!" exclaimed Brittany. "If *we* didn't steal it, then who did? If we can figure out who stole the venom, then we'll know who the killer is!"

"You read too much Sherlock Holmes as a child," objected Kay. "It's not our job to figure it out. Leave it to the police."

"If we leave it to the police," Brittany retorted, "then *you're* the prime suspect. Does that make you happy? You threatened Grant and now it turns out you could have stolen the venom. Not good. We'd better have some other ideas for them, don't you think?"

"Brittany's right," her mother agreed. "Unfortunately, it's not that simple. Christina and I both had access to the venom, of course, and I suppose almost anyone else at the zoo *could* have taken it. It isn't really guarded, or anything. And I can't say that someone didn't slip into the lab and take it."

"Terrific," Kay growled. "You just leave lethal doses of poison lying around? Why doesn't that make me feel better?"

"Kay!" Dr. Harlow warned. Then she shook her head. "It isn't just lying around. It's in my lab, which is locked when Christina isn't there, or I'm not. It's in the refrigerator, so it's out of sight. I never thought we'd have to worry about its being stolen. Zoos aren't top on anyone's list for break-ins, you know."

"All right," said Kay, simmering down. "Anyway, my other question: If whoever killed Grant did it by injecting him with the venom, wouldn't Grant have been a little bit worried? I mean, he'd hardly have stood there and let the killer inject him, would he? And Brittany didn't hear a fistfight, only a verbal argument. Right?"

"Yes," Brittany agreed slowly. "I *did* hear a slamming sound, but that must have been Grant hitting a locker as he fell because that was after he'd screamed." She frowned. "And, anyway, that would account for only one of the puncture marks in his neck, not both. Where did the other one come from?"

Dr. Harlow sighed. "I'm afraid I might be able to answer both questions at once. The venom wasn't the only odd thing in Grant's blood. Dr. Vitelli found another substance when he was doing the autopsy. He's not sure exactly what it is, but it seems to be some kind of steroid. It seems that Grant must have been taking steroids regularly to build himself up."

Brittany wished she didn't believe it, but it sounded right. Grant valued winning over everything. That he had been taking steroids really didn't shock her. "So maybe whoever killed him was the person he'd been getting steroids from," she guessed. "He could have been injected with the steroids and then the venom while he wasn't expecting it. Clever."

Kay smiled. "Then that rules *both* of us out, doesn't it? We don't know anything about drugs at all."

"You think the police will accept our word for that?" asked Brittany.

They didn't.

Sergeant Kahn turned her dark eyes on Brittany, openly suspicious. "So you came to tell us you weren't involved in stealing the venom?"

Brittany winced under the woman's glare. "It was my mom's idea," she said. "She thought it would help."

"I see." The detective spun in her chair, her icy gaze passing over Brittany, Kay, Dr. Harlow, and Christina, who had met them at the precinct house. "All four of you are here to tell me that you didn't kill Grant Witney, is that it?"

"All four?" Dr. Harlow asked, puzzled. "I don't understand. We're just trying to assure you that neither my daughter nor Kay is responsible—"

From behind them Sergeant Jellicoe spoke up. He seemed to enjoy standing behind people and talking. "I'm afraid you haven't realized something, Doctor. You and Ms. Ash must be considered suspects because you both had the best access to the venom."

"And," purred Sergeant Kahn, "both of you were at the school the day Witney died."

Dr. Harlow nodded. "But that was coincidental," she objected. "We were there for a school program, not to kill a student! Anyway, we were together the whole time, so we can alibi each other."

"I'm afraid not," Christina said apologetically. "If you recall, we left separately. I had my car with me."

"Your date!" exclaimed Dr. Harlow. "I'd forgotten about that!"

"I wish I could," muttered Christina. "It was a real washout."

"So what you are saying," Jellicoe observed, "is that either of you *could* have stayed at the school and killed Grant Witney?"

Christina turned to look at him, annoyed. *"Theoretically,* I suppose, but why would we have done so? And how could we have gone back into the school and killed him without being seen?"

Sergeant Kahn grimaced. "I didn't say we could account for all the facts. I'd like to be able to account for *some* of them, in fact."

Brittany's curiosity was roused. "What do you mean?"

"I mean," the woman replied, tapping a file folder on her desk, "that this murder gets more and more puzzling by the second. I appreciate your honesty and your theory, Dr. Harlow, but it doesn't fit the facts. Dr. Vitelli gave me a full autopsy report just before you came in."

"What do you mean?" Dr. Harlow asked. "Wasn't it the venom that killed him?"

"Oh, yes, it was venom, without a doubt. It's the only thing without a doubt. According to Dr. Vitelli, there was venom damage in *both* injection sites. If, as you theorized, the killer shot Witney with steroids first, then only the second puncture hole should have venom damage to the cells, right?"

"That's right," agreed Dr. Harlow. "There *was* urticaria about both holes. How stupid of me not to recall!"

"Urti-what?" asked Kay.

"A rash caused by the toxic effects of venom," Christina explained helpfully.

"But this makes it even crazier," objected Brittany. "You mean that the killer somehow managed to inject Grant *twice* with venom? And he stood there for it?"

"Apparently so," Jellicoe said dryly.

"Not only that," added Kahn. "The injection wasn't even given with a needle."

"What?" That was all four of them together.

"According to Dr. Vitelli," the detective said, "the tissue wasn't marked by a straight needle. The pathway was curved, like that from the fang of a snake. Two fangs, in fact."

"But that's utter nonsense!" exclaimed Dr. Harlow. "No snake could have injected that much poison into a person."

"Besides which," objected Christina, "from the spacing of the two puncture marks, the fangs would have been a good three inches apart! You're talking about a snake that's larger than any known to science!"

"That's right," Brittany's mother agreed. "To be capable of making a bite like that, you'd need a snake about twenty feet long!"

Kahn nodded. "But there *are* such snakes," she pointed out. "Boa constrictors, for example."

"Constrictors, yes," said Dr. Harlow. "They wrap around their victims to crush them to death. Poisonous snakes don't need to be so long. The largest vipers are only about four feet long. The largest poisonous snake in the world, the Australian Bushmaster, is never more than ten feet long."

"You see what I mean, then," Kahn said. "We have a lot of questions about this murder—and apparently too many answers to the questions we aren't asking."

CHAPTER

7

~≈~

As they walked out to their cars, Brittany shook her head. "It's getting more and more confusing," she admitted.

"Yes," agreed Christina. She rubbed the back of her neck. "And it sounds like the police are just as confused as we are. They *must* be, to have told us all that."

"Unless," objected Kay, "they did it for a reason. That Sergeant Kahn strikes me as very sneaky."

"Takes one to know one," Brittany said.

For once Kay didn't joke back. Instead she just wound a piece of hair around her finger. "I think she told us what she did to see what reaction she'd get. I wonder what she's after?"

"The killer, obviously," Dr. Harlow said. "I'll see you in the morning," she said to Christina. "Thanks for all of your help."

"What help?" her assistant answered, shrugging. "We don't seem to have discovered anything helpful —except that we need a lock for the refrigerator. 'Night, girls." With a wave she headed across to where she'd parked her car.

Brittany was deep in thought as her mother drove. Kay had to poke her twice to snap her out of it. "Hmm?"

"I've been talking to you for ten minutes and you're not even listening," Kay complained.

"It's never bothered you in the past," Brittany told her. "You just like me to be present when you sound off. I didn't know I was supposed to *listen*, too."

"Gee, thanks. What a friend. What were you thinking about that took all your concentration?"

Brittany chewed at her lip. "Just an idea. Did you ever read the Sherlock Holmes story called 'The Speckled Band'?"

"Hey, if it doesn't have pictures, I'm not interested," Kay replied.

Rolling her eyes, Brittany explained. "In the story the villain trains a snake to kill people. I wonder if something like that happened here? Maybe there wasn't another *person* in the locker room but a snake. A snake could easily slide in and out of that small window."

"Honestly," said her mother, "sometimes you do talk such nonsense. In the first place, that's just a story. While it may be a good story, it's certainly wildly inaccurate when it comes to snake behavior. Training a snake to kill is sheer nonsense. It's like any other creature—it kills for food, for self-defense, or out of fear. No snake would go out of its way to attack a person. And," she added, "it still doesn't explain how Grant had so much venom in his body. No single snake could have delivered it, and if there had been thirty or forty snakes in the locker room, I think you'd have noticed."

Brittany blushed. "I guess it was a pretty dumb theory."

"Wait a minute, though," Kay said. "Maybe it's an unknown species of snake. Is that possible?"

Dr. Harlow considered the idea for a moment. "I wouldn't say that we've discovered all the snake species in the world," she admitted, "but we certainly know all the ones in North America. New snakes would have to come from the tropics. So you'd have to assume that *if* the killer used an unknown snake, then whoever it was must have been in the tropics recently, been a bright enough naturalist to notice an unidentified snake, and to have been able to discover how deadly it was. Then, rather than notifying anyone, that person smuggled the snake back into the country and hid it away for the sole purpose of killing Grant. It's not very likely, is it? And, besides, there's still the *amount* of venom involved. A snake uses only enough to kill its victim. Why the massive overkill?"

"Okay, let's forget that thought," said Kay. "We're not getting anywhere, are we?"

"Of course we are," Brittany insisted. "Back to Sherlock again—eliminating the false theories will eventually leave us with the right one."

"Only if we've *thought* of the right one," Kay replied.

Dr. Harlow turned the car onto her street and frowned. "Hello," she muttered. "Now, who can that be?"

The girls followed her gaze. Outside the pleasant Dutch colonial house that the Harlows lived in was a parked car. They could make out two people inside the red Voyager. It wasn't at all familiar to Brittany. Dr. Harlow pulled into the driveway. As the three of them were getting out of the car, two people jumped out of the Voyager.

"Dr. Harlow!" the older one called. "Just a moment, please!" He and his companion hurried across to the small group. Brittany examined him as he rushed toward them. He was past middle age and balding. She'd never seen the man before.

"Do I know you?" Dr. Harlow asked icily.

"Jeff Chaney," the man said, puffing slightly as he drew up to them. He looked as if he lived on junk food. Judging from the stains on the sleeves of his jacket, he probably did. "I'm with the *News.*"

"Well, we all have our crosses to bear, Mr. Chaney," she told him. "If you'll excuse me?" She glared at him, but he didn't move.

"I just wanted to ask you a couple of questions, Doc," he persisted.

"Then call me and make an appointment," she said frostily, walking up to her door. "And I shall be able to make my 'No comment' official. Do you understand me?"

"Have a heart, Doc," he begged. "I got a living to make."

"So do I," Dr. Harlow answered. "And I am not responsible for whatever you chose to fritter your life away upon. And don't call me *Doc;* it's very irritating."

While her mother was arguing with the older man, Brittany glanced at his companion. He was a much younger man, about her age, or at most a couple of years older. He was slim and tall and seemed ready to leap into action at any second. He was handsome in a quirky kind of way, with a slight grin tugging at the corners of his mouth. He had dark hair, very thick and curly. He seemed amused by Brittany's mother's responses, but his dark eyes were firmly focused on Brittany. She found herself blushing under his stare, which made him go further and wink at her. Brittany tore her eyes away from his face and looked at Kay, who was staring at her with a very surprised expression.

"All right, *Doctor,*" said Chaney amiably enough. "I

apologize for riling you. But how about something I can use?"

"A brain, perhaps?" her mother snapped, slipping her key into the door. "It's too much to hope that the reason for your intrusion has nothing to do with a young man's murder? Or that you've decided to educate your readers about snakes?"

"They'd rather read about murders," he pointed out. "That's news. Most people don't like snakes."

"As I suspected. Good day, Mr. Chaney. Please leave immediately. And take your friend with you." She opened the door, ready to march inside.

Chaney glanced at the younger man. "He's not my friend," he said. "He's my assistant."

"Chad Curran," the young man said politely. His eyes flickered briefly to Dr. Harlow, and then returned to Brittany. She was looking at him again and blushed once more to be caught. He laughed, amused. "You must be her daughter, Brittany."

"You may be well mannered," Dr. Harlow told him, "but you're still unwelcome. If you'd please leave."

"Of course," Chad agreed pleasantly. He turned to his boss. "I think we'd better go, Jeff."

Chaney glowered at the three women, then shrugged. He spun around and waddled back to his car. Chad grinned again at Brittany.

"See you around." It wasn't politeness, Brittany realized—it was a promise. To her extreme annoyance, she couldn't stop blushing. The idea of seeing him again definitely excited her. There was something . . .

She dragged her attention back and saw Kay staring at her with a quizzical expression.

"I'd say you made a conquest," her friend said. Brittany could hear the tinge of irritation in Kay's voice. "He couldn't take his eyes off you." Kay wasn't used to being ignored.

"I wouldn't say that," Brittany replied.

"Wouldn't you?" Kay asked, her voice a little strained. "Why not?" Then she laughed, but it sounded forced. "Well, I'd better get home, before my folks think I *have* been arrested." She flounced down the driveway without a backward glance.

"Oh, dear," said Brittany. It was obvious that Kay was upset with her, and it wasn't her fault. She hadn't done anything to encourage Chad Curran. On the other hand, she hadn't done anything to discourage him, either. She did like the idea of meeting him again. He looked bright, pleasant, and handsome— and it was pretty obvious that he felt the same way about her. She couldn't imagine why he preferred her to Kay; and it was clear from Kay's response that she couldn't understand it, either.

"Don't let it bother you," her mother said. "I'm sure Kay'll get over her jealousy."

"Kay jealous of me?" asked Brittany. "You've got to be joking! Why would she be?"

Her mother gave her a shrewd look. "Well, at least you're not vain," she said. "But sometimes I wonder how bright you are. Stop putting yourself down for a change and start looking on the positive side. You're pretty, quite intelligent, and pleasant. As for Kay—

well, she's not a bad person, but she *is* vain and rather shallow. And she never tries to control her temper."

Brittany smiled. "Thanks for trying to cheer me up, but you're my mother and bound to be a bit prejudiced in my favor."

Her mother shook her head. "I know you're as blind as a bat without your glasses, dear, but try not to be mentally blind as well." She sighed as she went inside. "I guess we should grab something to eat."

Feeling pretty exhausted, Brittany followed her in. She wasn't sure what her mother was talking about. How could she seriously believe that *Kay* of all people was jealous of her? On the other hand, Chad Curran had paid careful attention to *her* . . . and it had felt really good. Maybe he had had an ulterior motive? Brittany knew she was out of her depth. Shaking her mind free of that train of thought, she went to see if she could help her mother.

Brittany was dreaming. It was one of those dreams where you *knew* it was only a dream, but it was still impossible not to react. She was standing in some sort of jungle clearing, with hissing, scratching, howling sounds all about her. Overhead, there was a droning sound, and as she stared upward, a huge aircraft came spinning down out of the sky straight toward her. Fire was spitting from it.

She wanted to run, but her feet felt rooted to the spot. Her legs refused to move, no matter how she strained. It was as if she were wrapped in rope, unable to do anything but struggle and whimper. In a huge ball of fire the aircraft slammed into the ground. A rolling fireball engulfed her, and Brittany finally managed to scream as she awoke.

But she *still* couldn't move.

Every inch of her skin was cold and damp with sweat. She could barely swallow and was unable to open her eyes. There was a nauseated sensation in her stomach, and she could feel every hair on her body standing up.

Was she still dreaming?

No; she was definitely awake. This was far too vivid to be a dream. She could feel the breath fluttering in and out of her nostrils as she breathed, and a constriction in her chest. But she was completely unable to move a muscle. Panic welled up in her, but there was no outlet for it. She was utterly paralyzed, not even able to whimper.

There was a soft noise. She couldn't open her eyes to see anything, so there was no telling what it had been. It sounded as if something was in her room, moving around slowly. Had someone broken in? What was happening? She tried to fight down the growing terror and concentrate on listening.

For a moment she heard nothing. Then there was the sound of something or someone moving again. It sounded closer. She realized that it had been coming from the direction of her window and was inching slowly toward the bed.

She fought her paralyzed muscles, striving just to

open her eyelids, so she could see. But it was no use. What was happening to her? Why couldn't she move? Was she in danger? What was—

Now there was a swishing sound, and then she felt something on her bed. The mattress buckled as *something* or someone moved onto the end of her bed. The sheets were pulled tighter across her legs, but she was still incapable of reacting. It was as if her body had been turned to stone . . .

Just as Grant's had been.

There was a slight movement, and Brittany felt the *whatever* slipping closer. The bed rocked slightly.

Then there was a soft rap at the door. "Brittany?" she heard her mother call out. "Are you okay, honey?"

With an explosion of motion, whatever was on her bed leaped away. The bed rocked, and the paralysis vanished. With a cry of terror and panic Brittany shot upright, her eyes springing open.

There was a vague shadow of movement at the window, the sound of something crashing in the bushes outside, before her door was flung open.

Her mother switched on the light and stood in the doorway, startled and confused, her old robe wrapped around her, her hair disheveled. "Brittany! What's wrong?"

Shaking, trembling, and on the verge of throwing up, Brittany couldn't respond. She could only point.

The window, which she generally left open an inch or so at night, was now open about six inches. The screen was gone.

Her mother crossed to the window and slammed it shut. Then she locked it. "What is it, honey?" she asked, crossing to the bed. "Something outside scare you?" She sat beside Brittany, who grabbed her and held her tightly for comfort.

"Something *inside*," she managed to gasp finally. "There was something in here with me. On the bed."

"What?" Dr. Harlow stared at her in shock. "Are you sure? You weren't dreaming?"

"Absolutely," Brittany told her. "I was wide awake, but I couldn't move. It was . . ." She shuddered. Then she pushed herself up and out of her mother's grip. She padded across her room to the window. "Something came in." In the soft light from her room she could see the garden outside her bedroom. The missing screen was down below. There were several holes in it, as if someone had wrenched it free by hand. And the plants below her window were broken and crushed. "Look."

Her mother stared down at the wreckage. "There *was* something here," she agreed. "Maybe one of Mrs. Noble's cats? They're destructive little creatures. One *could* have climbed in, I guess."

"It wasn't a cat," Brittany said with conviction. "It was . . ." She shook her head. "I don't know *what* it was. I've never felt like that. I couldn't move or . . ." Her voice trailed off. "Wait a minute!" she exclaimed. "I *have* felt like that before." The memory of the previous time came flooding back to her. "Right before Grant was killed. In school—I felt the same way. Like there was something crawling over my skin. I couldn't move or anything then, too. It was horrible."

"You never told me about this," her mother said.

"I didn't think it was relevant," Brittany admitted. "It was just too strange. But now . . ." She stared out her window. "Now I'm not so sure."

"Maybe you're ill," her mother suggested. "Nerves or something."

"No," Brittany insisted. "This wasn't *me*. It was something outside of me. I'm sure of it." She stared at her mother. "I felt something on my bed, Mom. It wasn't a cat. It was too heavy for that. It felt like a *person*. That heavy." She glanced at the window. "But nobody could have come in through such a narrow gap. Not even a contortionist. And how could anyone have made me feel like that?" She shivered at the memory of the cold, clammy paralysis.

Her mother studied her in concern. "I still think we should get you looked over by a doctor," she said. "But I guess that can wait till morning." She hugged Brittany. "You want to spend the rest of the night with me?"

"Yeah." The thought of sleeping in her own bed wasn't too appealing. "It would make me feel better."

"It would make *both* of us feel better," her mother added.

CHAPTER

8

As Dr. Harlow dropped Brittany at school the following morning, she gave her daughter an encouraging pat. "I'm going to look into getting an alarm system for the house today," she told her. "I've been meaning to do it for a while, and after last night . . ." She didn't have to finish that line of thought.

Brittany nodded. "Sounds like a good idea," she agreed. A flash of bright red hair caught her eye as Kay hurried up to her.

"I'm sorry I was such a grouch yesterday," Kay said. "It was one of those days, let's face it."

Maybe she was being a little overcritical, but Brittany didn't think that was much of an excuse. It had been just as bad a day for her. Still, there was no point in starting another argument. "Wasn't it?" she agreed. "And a weirder night, too." She told Kay about her strange intruder.

"You think this is linked to Grant's death?" Kay asked, frowning.

"I don't know," Brittany admitted. "But it would be a bit of a coincidence if someone or something picked last night to try to sneak into my room, wouldn't it? And through a small window, just like in the locker room."

Kay shrugged. "Maybe it was that Curran guy," she suggested. "He acted like he had the hots for your bod yesterday."

Brittany blushed. "I don't think so." Did she mean she didn't think her intruder had been Chad? Or that he wasn't interested in her? She didn't want to probe her own thoughts too much.

Kay stopped dead in her tracks. "Well! Speak of the devil!" Brittany followed her gaze to see Chad Curran standing by the main entrance, a lopsided grin on his face. Kay pouted. "Your boyfriend awaits," she said mockingly.

"He is *not* my boyfriend!" snapped Brittany, perhaps a shade too loudly.

"Oh?" asked Kay, her cool tone returning. "Does *he* know that?"

Chad hurried over to meet them. "Hi," he said, looking Brittany in the eyes. "I was hoping to see you."

"Waiting to see her," Kay corrected.

"Guilty as charged," admitted Chad, not at all abashed.

"Shall I leave the two of you lovebirds alone?" Kay asked, ice dripping from her voice.

Chad grinned at her. "How thoughtful of you," he replied, ignoring her hostility. "We'd appreciate that."

Brittany wanted to contradict him, but for some reason she couldn't bring herself to do it. She realized that she wanted to talk to Chad alone. It both excited and scared her. Kay threw them one last, frosty look and then flounced off into school.

"I've been thinking about you all night," Chad said abruptly. "How would you like to go out this weekend?"

Brittany was irritated when she blushed again. "I hardly know you," she protested.

"True," Chad agreed readily. He grabbed her hand, bowed, and kissed it. "Allow me to introduce myself: Chad Curran, reporter trainee and knight errant, at your service." He didn't let go of her hand.

Brittany found herself extremely attracted by his mixture of gallantry and nonsense. She said: "Can I have my hand back—if you've finished with it?"

"If you must," he replied, giving a theatrical sigh. "I was enjoying holding hands with you. It seemed like a good idea to practice, so I'm good at it later."

"Who said there was going to be a later?" she countered, pulling her hand free.

"Well, you didn't say there wouldn't be a later," he replied. "So I'm assuming that the answer is yes."

"It isn't," Brittany said. "I'm busy."

"I didn't set a time." He didn't seem at all put off.

"I'm *always* busy," Brittany told him.

"Then what you need is another hand," he replied cheerfully, holding his hands up. "And I've got two spares. What do you want me to do?"

"Go away." Brittany felt herself torn as she said it, but she didn't want to back down.

"Really?" Chad acted as if he didn't believe her. "You want me to leave, never to romance you again?"

"Yes," she insisted, though she was by no means as certain as she sounded.

"Ah, I love a girl who plays hard to get." The grin never left his face.

"I don't *play* hard to get," Brittany informed him. "I *am* hard to get."

"I've heard that," Chad agreed. Seeing her surprised expression, he added, "I've been waiting here awhile. I asked about you. Everybody told me to forget it—that you *never* date. Is that true?"

Brittany glared at him, both annoyed that he'd asked around and pleased that he was interested enough to do so. "I've never met anyone worth dating."

"Well, now you've met me, so it's not true anymore." He seemed totally serious in his self-praise. "I may only be a lowly reporter now, but you wait: I'll be *famous* lowly reporter one day. Maybe win the Pulitzer prize. Maybe even a Nobel. Maybe even your hand."

The word *reporter* triggered something inside Brittany. "So *that's* it," she snapped. "You want to date me just to get an inside line on this murder for your stupid paper!" How could she have been so blind as to think he really liked her? She felt angry and betrayed.

Chad's smile vanished completely. "Wrong," he said, sounding almost angry. "I want to date you because you're *you*. I promise, I will *never* talk about this murder unless you want."

"How can I believe that?" Brittany asked. Her certainty was crumbling, though.

"If I wanted to date a girl to get close to this story," Chad answered, "I'd have picked Kay, not you."

"Because she's prettier," said Brittany.

"No, she isn't." Chad abruptly grinned again. "I can't say she doesn't have a pretty face or a nice body. But I think you're the gorgeous one."

"Then you need glasses far worse than I do," Brittany said.

"Nope," Chad said, shaking his head. "But maybe you need different glasses so you can see yourself better. The reason I'd go for Kay is that she's not as bright as you. She'd let things slip. But not you. When you speak, it's carefully thought out and intelligent. Kay just lets fly with whatever is on her mind— usually nonsense."

"How do you *know* that?" demanded Brittany. "You've barely spoken to either of us."

He grinned again. "Hey, I'm psychic. It helps in my business. I see the future . . ." He waved his hand in the air. "I see . . . the two of us, blissfully married, with children all over the place, and—"

"No, you don't!" yelled Brittany, with far more volume and anger than she felt. She was probably more startled by her outburst than Chad was.

"Okay, I was just joking about being psychic," he admitted, taking a step back. "Don't get so bothered about it." Then his eyes narrowed and he stared at her thoughtfully. "Whoa there, that's not it . . ." Abruptly he asked: "Why do you wear those glasses?"

"Huh?" Brittany couldn't follow that question. "Because I'm blind without them. Why? Don't you like them?"

"They're fine," Chad answered. "They make you look even more intelligent. Puts some guys off, doesn't it? But I *like* intelligent women. Why don't you wear contacts?"

"I tried," Brittany told him. "But they irritated my eyes."

"Did they?" He didn't sound too sure he believed her. "Or is it that old saying that guys don't make passes at girls who wear glasses?"

Brittany stared at him, puzzled. "What do you mean?"

"I'm not altogether sure," he admitted. "Just a hunch. I'm not psychic, but I'm not stupid, either.

The glasses, the self-depreciation, and the business about hanging around with Kay. You picked her because she's so flamboyantly attractive, didn't you? It takes people's attention away from you."

"I don't know what you're talking about," she snapped, irritation growing inside her. "Kay's my friend."

"I'm sure she is—but I'll bet that's not all." Chad had clearly fixed his mind on something now. "You're trying to put boys off, aren't you? The glasses, hanging around with such an obvious flirt, and pretending you don't know how attractive you are."

"I'm *not* pretending!" Brittany replied hotly. "You're crazy if you think that."

Chad simply stared at her. "You're avoiding boys," he said finally. "Not just me, but all of them. That's why you never date."

"Why would I want to do such a stupid thing?" Brittany asked. She felt angry . . . and just a little scared.

"I don't know," Chad admitted. "But I *will* find out. Anyway," he said, grinning again, "you can easily prove me wrong."

"How?"

"Agree to go out with me."

Brittany studied him. "That way, you win anyway."

"I know," he admitted. "I love this one: Heads I win, tails you lose."

"Very well," she said finally. She held up a finger. *"One* date. One time. Then you leave me alone."

81

"It's a deal," Chad agreed. "Pick you up at six on Friday. Don't eat first." Then he grinned. "And if, after that, you tell me to stay away from you, I will."

"You can count on it," Brittany told him. Laughing, he loped away, waving back at her as he went.

Biting her lower lip, Brittany wondered if she'd just agreed to the smartest move of her life—or the dumbest. Refusing to think about it, she marched into school.

Waiting just inside the door was Kay. "I'm sorry, Brit," she said and then grimaced. "Geez, I'm constantly apologizing this morning, aren't I? I guess I let my temper win out again."

It did seem to be getting to be a habit with Kay, Brittany realized. Normally Kay never apologized for anything. "Take me as I am" was her usual motto. "It's okay, Kay," she replied. "We're both under a lot of stress, aren't we?"

"Yeah." Kay seemed glad of the excuse. "So, what's the verdict? *Is* he your boyfriend?"

"No!" Brittany protested. "Well . . . I agreed to one date. And one only."

"Really?" Kay studied her, and Brittany couldn't meet her friend's eyes. "That's a bit of a departure for you, isn't it? You usually squirm out of any date pretty fast."

"I don't want to talk about it," Brittany said, a shade angrier than she had intended. "Let's drop the subject, okay?"

"Touchy this morning, aren't you?" replied Kay. "Okay, let it go."

Despite Brittany's worries, the next two days passed fairly peacefully. Workmen came to the house to install an alarm system, but there was minimal fuss made over it. There was just the pain of having to remember to set the code when she left the house and to punch in the code if she was home first. She did feel better knowing that it was there, and that if anyone tried to break in again, the police would come.

Nobody tried anything, and the police stayed out of her life, too. She saw Sergeant Kahn at school once, talking to the coach, but there was no other sign of a police investigation. Kay seemed a lot more cheerful, too. The friction between them died down, and it was like old times.

The only incident that was even mildly out of the normal was the day that Brittany had to stop by Curtis's house to return some borrowed dishes. His family lived a couple of blocks from Brittany and her mom, on the edge of a small wood. Her uncle Joe was her late father's older brother, and he and Aunt Helen had a mess of kids—*mess* being the operative word. Their house was always untidy, no matter how often her aunt Helen blitzed it. As usual, she was cleaning when Brittany arrived. Two of her cousins—Timmy and Jacquie—were home, fighting over the TV in the den. Brittany got along better with them than with Curtis, but they were still too wild and noisy for her.

"It's a madhouse," Aunt Helen said with a sigh. "Then again, it always is." Taking the dishes from Brittany, she started to stack them in a kitchen cupboard. As Brittany turned to go, she paused to pet the family's calico cat, Buttons. Her aunt called out to her.

"Brittany . . ." She was obviously very uncomfortable. "Can I ask you something?"

After a moment's silence Brittany nodded, puzzled. "Sure."

Aunt Helen paused again, then plunged ahead, "Is everything all right at school? I mean, this Grant Whoozit killing and all."

"I guess," Brittany said. "What do you mean?"

"Well . . ." Aunt Helen sighed again and brushed a strand of hair out of her eyes. "It's Curtis. He's been really moody since Grant's death, and acting . . . well, *odd.*"

"Oh." To be honest, Brittany had always felt that Curtis was odd—and obnoxious. But she knew better than to say that.

"Has he been that way at school?" her aunt asked anxiously. "He seems to be obsessed with his weight lifting. Determined to be better than Grant was, or something." She spread her hands helplessly. "He's off tomorrow to some competition that he's been practicing like crazy for. I hardly see him at all."

"I don't see him much, either," Brittany replied. "Nobody at school's mentioned anything." She did remember how that one day she and Kay had been scared and puzzled by his fanaticism. "He's probably just overreacting to Grant's death. They *were* pretty close."

"I wonder how close," Aunt Helen said.

Brittany frowned. "What do you mean?"

"Well . . ." Aunt Helen shook her head. "According to the newspapers, Grant was taking steroids. I don't want to think that Curtis might be, too."

Brittany was astonished that thought had never occurred to her. *Was* Curtis taking steroids? Was that how he had managed to improve his lifting powers? Or was it just that he'd been determined to be better than Grant? She didn't know. He *might* be taking drugs, but there was no proof of it, and even to hint that she thought it possible would only upset her aunt more.

"I don't think he's doing anything like that," she managed to lie. "But I'll keep my ears open at school to see if I hear anything."

"Thanks, sweetheart," Aunt Helen said. "God, I hate thinking things like that about my own son, but—well, these days they say you can never be sure who's taking drugs."

Brittany managed to make some sort of polite reply and fled back home to think.

Was Curtis using steroids? She remembered Kay saying that Curtis had some odd mark on his neck, just like the fatal wound on Grant's neck. Was that where the drug was administered? She wasn't sure, but she felt pretty sure that steroids were pills that you took, not injected. None of it made much sense to her.

The phone rang, and she almost collapsed from shock, startled out of her dark thoughts. It was her mother.

"I'll be home late tonight," Dr. Harlow said. "Christina's had the afternoon off, and I'm a bit behind. Don't forget to set the alarm when you leave, will you?"

"Leave?" asked Brittany, puzzled. "Where am I going?"

Her mother chuckled. "Don't tell me you've forgotten your date?"

"Ohmigod!" gasped Brittany. "It's *Friday!*" She *had* forgotten somehow!

"Well, you're still aware of that at least. Have fun, honey." The line went dead.

Brittany stared at the receiver. How could she have forgotten her date? Had she been so distracted? Or . . . had she *deliberately* tried to forget about it? She did want to go out with Chad—didn't she? She was kind of excited by him, so why was there also this feeling of utter dread in her heart?

CHAPTER
9

Rushing into her room, Brittany checked on the time. Past five-thirty! Chad was to pick her up at six, and she hadn't even started getting ready! She threw open her closet door and stared at her clothes. What to wear? She had no idea where they were going. Jeans and a T-shirt? A nice skirt and blouse? Where would Chad take her? He couldn't be making a huge amount of money, so nowhere *too* ritzy, that was for sure. On the other hand, he'd probably try to impress her so she'd agree to see him again.

Not that she had any intention of giving in on that point!

Finally she settled on a jersey top and a pair of slacks. That should be appropriate wherever they went—she hoped! Then she dashed into the bathroom to brush out her hair and touch up her makeup. She'd just clipped her hair back into a ponytail when the bell rang. Fighting down the waves of panic that threatened to sweep her away, Brittany managed to open the door.

It was Chad, as handsome as she recalled, his lazy grin intact. He was dressed casually, so Brittany had chosen right. In his hand he had a bunch of—she peered closely—heliotrope!

"Are they for me?" she asked, surprised and pleased.

"Actually," he confessed, "they're for your mother. Is she home?"

"Uh . . . no." Brittany wasn't sure how to react. She was a little disappointed.

Chad winked at her. "Put them in water, then, where she can see them. I hope she knows her Kate Greenaway."

"The Language of Flowers?" Brittany asked, puzzled. "We have a copy. Why?"

"Heliotrope means *respect and devotion.* It'll let her know my intentions toward you are honorable." He grinned. "Always reassure the parents when you're dating."

"Flatterer." But, despite herself, Brittany was pleased with the compliment. She fetched a vase, and he placed the flowers in it, then left the vase on the coffee table. As an afterthought, Brittany found her Kate Greenaway and left it beside the vase.

"Nice touch," he admitted. "Okay, are you ready?"

"I just have to set the alarm," she told him.

His eyes narrowed. "That's new, isn't it?"

She nodded. "How did you know?"

"There wasn't one when I stopped by the other day; I held back and watched you enter your house. When I was with Jeff Chaney, remember?"

"Oh, right." She ushered him out the door, then punched in the code and pulled the door closed behind her.

Chad looked worried. "Is it just coincidental that you've installed an alarm system? Or is there a problem?"

She evaded a direct answer. "Mom's been thinking about it for some time." To forestall further questions, she asked, "So, where are we going?"

"To a great little place I know. It's called Windward. Have you heard of it?"

"Nope."

"Trust me, you'll love it." He had a slightly battered-looking Toyota and held the door open for her. "It's fun."

Chad turned out to be exactly right. Windward was a small restaurant and club down by the lake. The food was wonderful, and afterward there was dancing. She couldn't remember the last time she'd danced so much, and she didn't want to stop, even though she was tired. Eventually, though, she collapsed happily into a seat and took a long drink of her Diet Coke.

"Happy?" Chad asked, his eyes sparkling in the low-level lighting.

Brittany nodded. "Very," she admitted. "It's a fun evening, thank you."

"Thank *you*," he told her. "I'm having more fun than you; after all, I'm here with the prettiest girl in the place and the rest of these guys aren't."

Brittany couldn't help laughing at his flattery. Her guard, for once, was down, and they chatted about everything. He was an only child, also, and he told her of his plans to become a writer. He'd skipped going to college to get experience in journalism. He was taking evening classes toward a degree, though. She told him of her plans to follow her mother into animal studies and veterinary medicine. To her growing alarm and delight, she discovered that she was completely under Chad's spell.

He kept his promise not to talk about Grant. They discussed music and literature—he liked many of the same performers and writers as Brittany. Finally he asked about her father.

"I don't want to upset you," he said. "If you'd rather not answer, don't."

"Nothing like that," Brittany replied. "He died when I was twelve, in a plane crash."

"I'm sorry," he said simply. "He must have been a really great guy."

"Why do you say that?"

"Well, he raised one terrific daughter, for one

thing." Chad grinned again. "And after seeing your mom handle Jeff Chaney the other night, I'm sure she'd never settle for any guy who wasn't her match in brains and personality."

"You really do have a silver tongue, don't you?" Brittany said, laughing.

"It's from the Irish side of the family," he assured her. "We're all full of the blarney." His smile faded. "Do you miss him?" he asked, abruptly serious.

She couldn't lie to him. "Very much," she admitted. "I had nightmares for years about it. I still do, sometimes."

He nodded. "Well, enough depression for one night, or you'll never go out with me again."

"Hey!" Brittany frowned. "I promised to go out once and that was all. Our once is just about over."

He looked glum. "Yeah, well, it's getting late. I'd better take you home." He led her outside. It was dark and slightly chilly. "So," he said a little too casually, "when can I see you again?"

"Haven't you been listening?" Brittany demanded. "I said one date, and you've had it. You said you wouldn't push it."

"Not quite," he corrected her, climbing in beside her. As he started the car up, he looked across at her. "I said that I wouldn't push it if you didn't enjoy it. So, be honest—did you enjoy it?"

Brittany considered lying, but she couldn't. "Yes," she finally said. "It's been a terrific evening."

"Then what's the problem?" He pulled out of the lot and started on the road home.

"I'm just not a dating kind of girl, I guess." She couldn't tell him about her feelings of panic and fear.

"Is that a fact?" He snorted, then pulled over to the side of the road. Turning to look at her, he challenged her. "Look me in the eyes and tell me you don't want to see me again. If you can do that, I promise never to bother you again."

Brittany gave a start. Was he serious? He was staring at her in a very unnerving fashion. She stared back and took a deep breath. All she had to do was tell him she didn't want to see him again.

All she had to do was *lie*. She *did* want to see him again, but she was terrified. She felt the conflicting emotions warring inside her. No words came out of her mouth.

"That's what I thought," he said, pulling back onto the road again. "You *do* want to see me again. Do you like cats?"

"Huh?"

"Cats," he repeated. "I've got to cover a cat show on Sunday, and I've been given a couple of free passes. Maybe you'd like to come along. If you don't want to look at me, you can always watch the fuzzy felines."

"A cat show?" She laughed. "That's not the way to win a Pulitzer!"

"Sure it is," he said, grinning. "The Pulitzer Cat Coverage Prize is *very* prestigious. Besides, Jeff's off following some leads of his own, and my editor wants me to keep busy."

"Leads?" asked Brittany. "Like what?"

Chad shrugged. "He said he'd done some research

into a couple of old cases out of town, and they set him thinking. Apparently he thinks better without me around, and I got stuck with the cats. So, will you come? Or will you tell me to get lost?"

Brittany paused, but finally said, "What time Sunday?" Why did it feel as if she was making a horrible mistake?

"Two. I'll pick you up at one-thirty." He said nothing for a short while, until they were almost back to her house. Then he added quietly, "If I were into cheap psychology, Brittany, I'd say you're scared of me."

"What?" Now she was completely confused. "Scared? What do you mean?"

"Well, not of me, exactly," he admitted. "Of any guy. That's why you go to such great lengths to scare us all away. You don't want to let anybody get too close. Do you?"

She felt light-headed. "I don't do that," she protested weakly.

"Yes, you do," he said firmly. "You admitted that you've enjoyed this evening, but you put up a stiff fight not to see me again. And there's only one reason I can think of for that." He pulled the car over again.

With a start, Brittany realized that they'd arrived at her house. Chad's eyes were fixed on her face, and giddiness swept over her. "And what's that?" she asked.

"That you feel just as mad about me as I feel about you. That you really want to keep on seeing me. And *that* scares the heck out of you."

"If that's true," she asked, "and I say *if*, then why would liking you scare me?"

"Because of your father," he said. "You're afraid to let any guy get close to you in case he leaves."

"That's crazy!" she protested, her throat tightening.

"No," he contradicted. "It's understandable. But it's wrong." Abruptly he leaned across and suddenly kissed her.

Caught completely off-guard, Brittany first wanted to pull away. Her muscles froze up on her, though, and she couldn't move or do anything but kiss him back.

Eventually he pulled free. "Well," he said, "I guess I'd better see you to the door. Your mother might come out here and bang on the windows."

"She'd never do that," Brittany informed him. She felt very light-headed now.

Chad grinned. "Shall we test that theory? I'll bet if we sat here and made out for another ten minutes, she'd come out."

Unable to help herself, Brittany laughed. "I think we'd better go with your first idea," she said. "Walking me to the door."

"That wasn't my *first* idea," he told her. "It was just the first one I said out loud." He winked at her, and then got out of the car. He walked her up to the door as he had promised. "I'll see you on Sunday? Or are you going to try to talk me out of it again?"

Brittany considered the idea. "No," she finally said. "It's a date." She wasn't at all sure how accurate his theories about her had been, but she was certain of one thing—she *did* want to see him again.

"Good night," he murmured. As he turned to go, she grabbed his arm.

"I do know what I want sometimes," she told him.

"Good," he said approvingly. "And what do you want?"

"This." She pulled him closer and kissed him. Finally she let him go.

"Whew," he murmured and leaned past her to ring the doorbell. "Don't make it any harder for me to leave," he begged.

The door opened and Brittany's mother was there. "Home already?" she asked, a smile on her face.

"She begged and begged to stay out all night," Chad replied. "But I brought her home anyway. Good night, Dr. Harlow."

As Brittany slipped inside, her mother laughed. "Well," she exclaimed, "he's certainly glib, isn't he?"

Brittany agreed breathlessly.

"So," her mom asked, closing the door, "when do you see him again?"

Brittany paused. "What makes you think I've agreed to see him again?"

"Young lady," her mother replied, "I've been in love. I can recognize those silly grins on your faces. You wouldn't look so happy if you hadn't planned to go out again."

Brittany blushed. "Sunday."

"Good." Her mother stroked her cheek. "He seems like a very personable young man. I like him."

"So do I," admitted Brittany honestly. "I like him an awful lot."

It had been a wonderful evening, but that night was one of the worst since the death of her father. Brittany awoke, shaking, sweating, and shivering with terror. For a panic-stricken moment she thought she was still asleep and dreaming, but then a flash of lightning and a crash of thunder set the house shaking. It was followed almost immediately by the flickering intensity of another close lightning bolt and clap of thunder that made her window rattle.

But the storm outside, even with the screaming wind and the hammering rain, was nothing compared to the one in Brittany's being. She couldn't recall the details of the nightmares she'd suffered through, but the nightmares had been filled with death and terror.

Chad's right, she realized. *I am terrified of letting him get close to me. I'm scared stupid that I'll lose him, too, and that would be more than I could take.* The thought of losing someone she loved as she had lost her father was too much to bear.

But what could she do?

CHAPTER
10

~

On Saturday morning she accompanied her mother to the zoo. She loved the zoo and its animals. Curiously, though, she'd never felt the urge to have a pet. But at the zoo she felt as though she and they were all part of an extended family. She wandered about for a while, peering in at the compounds and living areas. No cages, thank goodness! Most of them had been eliminated years back, and the animals were given room to roam. Instead of mesh or bars, glass walls separated the creatures from the public.

She headed for the Midnight World building, one of her favorite exhibits. Here were all the smaller animals that were crepuscular—sleeping during the day and waking to live and eat and play at night. In this building the lighting was dim by day and bright at night, fooling the animals on exhibition into thinking it was night during the day. Her mother and Christina sometimes worked in here, since there were several species of snakes and reptiles in the displays. Despite her mother's preference for snakes, Brittany liked mammals better. Her own choice was the fennec foxes. These small desert hunters with huge batlike ears stole her heart.

From the Midnight World, she crossed the Employees Only path to the Ophiology Department. The watching security guard knew her well enough to give her a nod and a wink and let her pass. Inside the laboratory Brittany found Christina, but not her mother.

The exotic assistant looked up from her work and smiled at Brittany. "Hi, Brit. Come to help out?"

"Sure," she agreed. "What's to do?"

"Well, we need to get the incubators ready," Christina told her. "The pit viper caught us by surprise and laid a clutch of eggs this morning. Your mother's collecting them right now."

"Can do," Brittany said. She moved to the small room that acted as a hatching area. There were several sets of incubators, two of them already in use. A third one had the glass top open and was obviously the one that Christina had started to get ready. Though the snakes might hatch their own eggs, Brittany knew that there was a good chance that the eggs could be destroyed. If someone rapped on the glass tanks, the mama snake might freak out and break the eggs. It was safer to hatch them in the incubators, where they could be monitored.

As Christina hooked up the monitoring equipment, Brittany cleaned off the glass top and the inside of the incubator to ensure there would be no germs. As she moved the glass aside, Brittany glanced across the room and saw the small fridge by the door.

"Is that where the venom is stored?" she asked.

Christina barely looked up, then nodded. "That's it." She gave a small smile. "And we've had a lock added, so you can't peek in." Then, realizing what she said might have been misconstrued, she added hastily, "I'm sorry. That was thoughtless of me. Forget I said it."

"That's okay." Brittany knew that Christina hadn't meant anything by her remark. "Did the police check it for clues?"

"Are you kidding?" Christina snorted. "They had so many people in here that your mom finally threw some out. She was afraid they'd push over the equipment. That stringy-looking policewoman—"

"Sergeant Kahn?"

"Yes, that's the one. She had her men taking fingerprints all over the room. She was really annoyed when she only turned up prints belonging to me, your mother, and the cleaner." Christina grimaced. "She seems pretty certain that your friend Kay is guilty. I think she'd really been hoping to find Kay's prints all over the fridge. Of course, I had to tell her that the cleaners had no doubt cleaned *after* the theft."

Brittany was annoyed. "Did you *have* to tell them that?" she asked.

Her annoyance must have shown. Christina looked at her rather sharply. "Brittany, you're a nice girl, and I think of you as my friend. But I must be honest—I do not like that Kay at all. She's a bad-tempered brat at the very least. I don't know if she really did kill that boy, but I am certainly not going to try to make her look good to the police."

"I didn't mean you should have *lied,*" Brittany answered, stung by Christina's comments.

"No, I'm sure you didn't," agreed the assistant. "Look, let's not argue about Kay, please? If you want to be friends with her, that's your decision. But don't ask me to cover for her."

"You *do* think she's guilty," accused Brittany.

"It seems to me to be a strong possibility, yes," Christina agreed. "But it's none of my business." She sighed and stood back from the incubator. "There, it's all ready. Thank you for your help, Brittany."

Then Brittany's mother arrived carrying a box with four eggs in it, and Brittany was too busy for a while to think about Christina's comments.

Brittany was reading at home that night when the phone rang. She was hoping it was Chad and felt vaguely disappointed when she heard Kay's voice. "Oh. Hi, Kay."

"So," Kay asked, "how'd it go?"

"What?"

"What do you mean *what?*" yelped Kay. "Your *date*, of course. I've been waiting for you to tell me about it. I finally couldn't stand it any longer."

Brittany laughed. "Oh, that. It went pretty well, thanks."

"And?"

"And *what?*"

"Jeez, Brittany," Kay complained. "Do I have to come over there and punch some answers out of you? Are you seeing him again?"

"Well, I did agree to go to a cat show with him tomorrow," Brittany admitted. "But nothing more than that."

"A *cat* show?" She could hear Kay shuddering. "That is not what I'd call major league romantic, Brit."

"It's for his job," Brittany explained. "But he wanted me around."

"Well, I'll give him marks for taste, anyway," Kay said. After a short pause she added, "This is weird, isn't it? You with a boyfriend and me without." There was an element of pain in her voice.

"Yeah, I guess," Brittany agreed. "Don't worry, though. I'm sure that the universe will return to normal pretty soon."

"Why? Are you going to give him his marching orders?"

Brittany finally clicked. "Kay!" she exclaimed. *"You* want to go out with him!"

"Well," said Kay defensively, "he *is* cute. And— forgive me for saying this—but he's kind of wasted on you. You don't know what to do with a hunk like him."

"Maybe not," said Brittany, annoyed at her friend's callousness. "But I *do* know what to do with a phone like this." She slammed the receiver down and stood glaring at it for a moment.

How *could* Kay? After all their years of friendship, how could she be so cruel? Brittany felt betrayed and furious. Was she finally starting to see the true Kay? One who would betray anyone to get what she wanted?

One who might even kill if it served her purposes?

CHAPTER

11

~~~

"I don't believe it!"

Brittany couldn't help laughing at the expression on Chad's face. "What can't you believe?" she asked.

"That there are this many cats in the world." He waved his hand around the Knights of Columbus Hall.

The whole place was filled with cats, cat owners, cat merchandise, and others along to look, admire, and buy. The hall was bursting at the seams with cats. "It is pretty incredible," Brittany agreed.

"Incredible?" He wrinkled his nose. "Speaking as a dog person, I'd say *disgusting* was a better word." He shook his head. "Cats are selfish, vain, preening creatures. This is what I get for being the lowest reporter on the totem pole. The editor tells me to cover a cat show, I cover a cat show. But I can't knock it. It might have been a flower show. I did one last month." He rolled his eyes. "Flowers are for gardens and giving girls. Or the girl's mom," he added. "Not for parading around shows."

"And what are cats for?" she asked.

"Roadkill," he replied, keeping a perfectly straight face.

Brittany giggled and punched him gently. She'd never been to one of these kind of shows before, and she was astonished at how much was happening. Close by the door were booths. People were selling anything and everything to do with cats—from carrying cases, combs, and collars to books, brushes, and baskets. There were ID disks, items of cat clothing, videos, posters, special license plates for cars, and collector's items such as pewter models.

Next came the exhibition areas and rings where the judging would take place. Beyond that was the area where the cat owners and exhibitors were camped out. There were whole rows of traveling cases and small cages. Many of them had trophies beside them already, along with photos and certificates.

Each of the cats was a purebred, that was for certain. There were felines of all shapes, sizes, and colors. Brittany knew a large number of breeds, but there were some that baffled her. Chad seemed totally out of his depth.

"Good grief," he muttered. "I don't even know where to start."

Brittany nodded toward the front of the hall. "Come on, let's go over to the exhibition area. I think the judging is about to start soon."

"I hate cats," muttered Chad, but he kept up with her. Abruptly he stopped dead in his tracks. "Whoa! Is that a cat or a bear?"

Brittany chuckled when she saw what he was staring at. It was a massive cat, the size and build of a medium-size dog. The fur was on the long side and a deep, rich brown. "That's a Maine coon cat," she told him. "It's the largest of the domestic breeds."

"I'll say." Chad was quite impressed. "It's almost nice enough to be a dog."

There was a sudden burst of static from the P.A. system, and then an announcer's voice. "Ladies, gentlemen, and cat fanciers, thank you for attending today. The first round will begin shortly."

"Perfect timing," Chad said. He led Brittany toward the judging area. "Opening ceremonies are about to begin." Brittany saw that several people, obviously judges, were gathered there. She gave a start.

Her cousin Curtis was there, too, looking rather self-conscious and uncomfortable.

Brittany turned to Chad. "What's Curtis doing here?" she asked.

"Didn't I mention he's going to give some of the cat

awards? Local sports hero, and all that. He won his competition yesterday pretty easily, I gather."

Unexpected anger flooded through Brittany. "You *promised* me that you weren't going to talk about the murder," she growled, keeping her voice low.

"What do you mean?" Chad asked, startled.

She didn't want to make a scene, but she felt betrayed by Chad. He had brought her with him just to get close to Curtis to learn more about the murder. "You *deliberately* didn't say anything about Curtis being here."

"And I *haven't* said anything about the murder," Chad replied, still off-balance. He looked at her. "Brittany, I didn't mention Curtis because I didn't see any reason to. I only asked you to come because I wanted you to be here with me."

"To get in with Curtis!" she snapped. "You wanted to use me to get information from him."

"No!" Chad glared at her. "Look, I wanted to be with you because I like being with you. Curtis has nothing to do with it. I will admit that when I heard he was going to be here, I hoped I could talk to him about the murder. I do have a job to do. I am a reporter. And I want to succeed. Is that wrong? If I can get a good story about what happened to Grant, then I may get a promotion. But I had no intention of using *you* as an inside source."

Her anger started to dissolve. She wanted to believe Chad, and he seemed to be telling her nothing but the truth. But was she just fooling herself? "Maybe we should talk," she suggested.

Chad nodded. He led her off toward the concession stands, a quieter area. "Okay," he said. "I promised I wouldn't discuss the murder with you unless you wanted to talk about it. I've been very careful to stick to my promise, Brittany. But you have to give me room to do my reporting."

Brittany sighed. "I know," she agreed. "I guess I was being unfair. It's just that . . ." She shrugged. "I was scared that you were only going out with me to use me."

"Don't even think that," Chad said. "I give you my word that the only reason I'm seeing you is pure selfish lust. Nothing to do with business."

Brittany couldn't help herself. She smiled. "You're impossible."

"Nope. Just *very* improbable." He looked into her eyes. "Am I forgiven?"

How could she refuse? "I guess," she agreed. "But next time *tell* me what you know in advance, okay?"

"I promise." Chad gestured back at the competition area. "Shall we go see?"

Brittany nodded. Together, they walked back. They were in time to catch the tail end of Curtis's rather fumbling welcome speech. He'd never been good with words, and he seemed to be terribly self-conscious. Brittany also realized that he seemed to be very, very nervous. Stage fright? Or something else?

There was a smattering of polite applause, and then the announcer came forward to start the first round of competition. Curtis, looking dreadfully uncomfortable, started to move away from the ring. As he did so, he came close to one of the competitors. Brittany could see that she was carrying a beautiful silver Persian, a gorgeous creature.

As Curtis came close, the cat abruptly reared up in its owner's arms. Fur rising, the cat screeched and spat at Curtis. As Curtis staggered back, the cat twisted free from its owner's arms and launched itself at Curtis.

He yelled as the cat's claws sank into his arm, and the animal tried to bite him. It was having a fit, hissing, spitting, and slashing at Curtis. Shaking his arm and crying out in pain, Curtis tried to send the cat flying. The cat sank its teeth into his arm, ripping at the muscle and sending bright flecks of blood flying.

With a scream Curtis finally flung the snarling, hissing feline across the ring. It landed heavily and yowled in agony.

Brittany stared at her cousin in shock. What had caused the cat to attack him like that? Curtis was clutching his bleeding arm. She could see blood welling up through his fingers. He'd been hurt rather badly.

"You'd better get to a doctor," Chad said, moving forward to help.

"Get the hell away from me!" Curtis yelled, and then whirled and ran for the exit. As he passed the other cats, Brittany heard a cacophony of hisses, howls, and screeches.

"Well," Chad said slowly as startled human voices

spoke up all around them. "That was definitely unusual, wouldn't you say?"

As Chad was driving her home, Brittany mulled over the events of the afternoon without coming up with any real answers. She and Chad had talked to several judges and winning cat owners and taken a whole roll of film. He'd done his duty for the paper. But she knew that the cat show wasn't the thing uppermost on his mind right now.

"Let's swing home past my cousin's house," Brittany suggested, breaking the silence in the car.

Chad raised an eyebrow. "You mean that? I don't want to pressure you. You know that."

"Yes, I *do* know that," she agreed. "It's my idea, so don't argue."

"No arguments," he replied. "So—why the sudden offer?"

"Because," she told him honestly, "I want some answers myself. Ever since Grant's death, there have been very strange things happening. The cat attack is just one more bewildering event." She looked at Chad. "I need to talk to somebody. No, I need to talk to you, or I'll go crazy. I may already *be* crazy."

He studied her with evident concern. "You're not crazy," he assured her. "But I'm more than willing to listen." He pulled the car over and shut off the engine.

Once she started, Brittany found it difficult to stop. She told Chad everything she knew about Grant and Curtis, and all her conversations, no matter how obscure they seemed to be. She even told him about the weird paralysis and terror she'd experienced twice. Finally she simply stared at him. "So, what's the verdict? You want to dump me now? *Am* I crazy?"

"No and no," he replied seriously, his voice strained. "There's definitely something odd going on here." He concentrated for a moment. "Okay, now I repay you for all that information. I talked with Sergeant Kahn. She's a real go-getter, you know. Not many women make it on a homicide squad, but she's very good. And she's determined to find Grant's killer. Kahn is convinced that your friend Kay is guilty. She's not stupid enough to come right out and say it, but it's there when she talks. She really wants to nail Kay. The problem is explaining how she *could* have killed Grant without being seen. Unless, of course, Curtis is lying to cover up for her."

"Do you think he is?" asked Brittany.

"He's covering up *something,*" Chad said. "I hate to say this, but he's the guiltiest-looking person I've ever seen. He's got a very bad case of the jitters. You saw him today. He'd just won a major championship in weight lifting and he should have been high. Instead, he looked like he'd been beaten up. It doesn't make sense."

"Do you think *he* killed Grant?"

"Maybe," Chad admitted. "After all, you saw him with his hand on Grant's body. But if he did kill Grant, he's the clumsiest killer imaginable." He shook his head. "I've got my own theories. Maybe they're wrong, but I don't think either Kay or Curtis killed Grant."

"Really?" Brittany felt better already. She hated the fact that she couldn't eliminate her suspicions about her best friend or cousin. If Chad could help, she'd be thrilled.

"I think that Grant was on steroids for a while. That's why he was so good with the weight lifting. And I think that Curtis knew it. Grant was probably killed by whoever supplied him with the steroids. I don't know how or how the attacker got away, but it had to have happened after there was some kind of argument." He slapped his head. "Or maybe you heard Curtis and Grant arguing. Curtis could have seen Grant with the drugs and wanted some. Grant could have refused. Anyway, Grant injected himself with what he thought were steroids—but his supplier could have switched the drugs for snake venom—then he fell over dead and hit the locker. Curtis may have realized what happened and hid the drugs and syringe before you got inside. Then, later, he confronted Grant's supplier and demanded steroids in return for his silence. It seemed more important to him to be a winner than to bring Grant's killer to justice. But now he's having second thoughts. Maybe his conscience is bothering him. Which would explain his nervousness."

Brittany snorted. "What conscience? Curtis doesn't have one. He's always been selfish and nasty. When I was a kid, he deliberately stuck my hand in an open lamp socket, to give me an electric shock. Just to see if I'd scream or cry." She shivered at the memory. "No, I think Curtis could have done just what you said. It's probably occurred to him that the killer might switch drugs on him, too, so each time he takes steroids, he must wonder if it's actually poison. That would make him very nervous, wouldn't it?"

Chad gave her a wide smile. "Brittany, I just love how intelligent you are. That makes perfect sense to me. Maybe we should team up to write this story." Then he pretended to think it over. "But I get to keep the Pulitzer!"

Blushing at his praise, Brittany said, "I'm not a writer. I do feel better having talked things over with you. On the other hand, there are a few things our theory doesn't explain."

"Such as?"

"Why that cat attacked Curtis at the show."

Chad shrugged. "Maybe he's not a cat person, and the cat knew it."

"That doesn't work," Brittany replied. "My cousins have owned a cat for years, and it's never avoided Curtis."

"Then maybe the steroids we think he's taking do something to Curtis that the cat sensed and didn't like," offered Chad. "You know, maybe a scent or something that only cats can pick up."

"Maybe." Brittany had an idea. "Maybe we can find out what Buttons thinks of Curtis at his house," she suggested.

"Buttons is their cat, I take it," Chad answered. He started the car again. "You've got a devious mind, and I love you for it."

Brittany felt a thrill when he said that. Even if he

wasn't being totally sincere, she liked him to say he loved her for any reason. "Also we haven't been able to explain what happened to me when I was paralyzed," she added. "Unless you think it was just my mind being more devious than usual."

"To be honest," he said, "I *can't* explain what happened to you. But I do believe *something* happened." He shook his head. "It's got me completely baffled. But I can't be expected to have answers for everything, can I?"

"No," she agreed, a little disappointed that he didn't have at least one bright suggestion to offer. She didn't like not being able to explain those weird episodes of freezing terror. She gave him directions to Curtis's house. "So you think that Kay had nothing to do with any of this?"

"It's hard to say," he replied honestly. "I mean, she was dating Grant for some time. Is it possible she didn't know he was taking steroids?"

"Kay?" Brittany laughed. "He could have had two heads, and she wouldn't have noticed. She tends to pay attention only to things that affect her directly."

"Yeah, I got the feeling that she was self-absorbed." After a little while Chad stopped the car. "This is the house?"

Brittany nodded. "Right. Come on, let's see if he's home." She led the way to the side door of the large, rambling house. She could hear her younger cousins playing in the backyard. Aunt Helen was, as usual, in the kitchen.

"Hi, Brittany," she said, more preoccupied than normal. "Who's your friend?"

"Chad Curran," Brittany informed her aunt. "We've come to talk to Curtis."

"You just missed him," her aunt replied. "He came home from the cat show in a bad mood, and then stormed out about ten minutes ago. I've got no idea where he went. Is it important?"

"It can wait," Chad assured her. "We can catch him at school tomorrow."

"Fine." Aunt Helen stared around the messy kitchen. "Where's that pie plate?" she muttered, her visitors already pushed to the back of her mind.

Brittany saw Chad put his fingers to his face and pull them away, pantomiming whiskers. Catching his meaning, she asked, "Where's Buttons?"

"Didn't you hear?" her aunt replied, pulling a pie plate from the stack beside the sink. "Buttons has been missing a day or so." She sighed. "I'm afraid he may have been run over."

"I'm sorry to hear it," Brittany said. She'd rather liked the old cat.

"It's a shame," Chad agreed. "Maybe that's what upset Curtis, worrying about the cat."

"It could be," agreed Aunt Helen. "Buttons acted very odd when he was around him the past few days."

Brittany felt a surge of excitement. "Hissing and growling, you mean?"

Her aunt reacted sharply. "Yes. How did you know?"

"We saw another cat act that way around him earlier today," Brittany replied. "It was the cat that attacked him on the arm."

"On the arm?" Aunt Helen sounded puzzled. "A cat attacked him? I didn't see any scratches or anything."

Chad frowned. "Are you sure? He was bitten and scratched and was bleeding pretty badly."

"I'd have noticed," Aunt Helen told him. "There was nothing wrong with his arm."

A chill gripped Brittany. "Nothing?" she asked hollowly. "But . . . how is that possible?"

Her aunt shrugged. "I guess it wasn't as serious as it looked," she said, dismissing it. "Now, I don't want to sound rude, but I do have a lot to do."

As they headed back to the car, Brittany turned troubled eyes to Chad. "He was badly scratched. We *know* he was. Aunt Helen's a bit flaky, but even she'd see it if Chad had a bandage on, or was bleeding all over the place."

"You'd think so." Chad sounded as shaken as she did. "So we've got more to check with Curtis. It does seem as if cats have taken a strong aversion to him. I wonder if Curtis had something to do with Buttons's disappearance? Also it seems as if Curtis can heal almost instantly."

"Yes," Brittany agreed slowly. "Whatever is going on here, I'm sure Curtis is right in the middle of it. Hey," she said, pointing, "that car looks very familiar somehow."

Chad followed her finger. There was a red Voyager

parked beside the small wooded area. "That's Jeff Chaney's car," he said in surprise. "I wonder what he's doing here?"

Brittany shrugged. "Maybe we should ask him. You said he was following up his own leads on the case."

Chad nodded. "Come on."

They walked quickly down the block. The road curved around the corner here, and then more or less petered out. The builders had originally planned more streets for the development, but had gone bankrupt. The area had been left woods. Brittany had played in them a lot when she was younger.

"Empty," said Chad at Jeff's car. He tried the door, which was unlocked. "He can't be far away, though. He usually locks his car." There was obviously only one place the reporter might have gone. "Would you like a walk in the woods?"

Brittany was a little curious, so together they moved onto the faint trail that led into the wood. It was easy going, and in less than a minute they had lost sight of the road. It was quite peaceful amid the trees and ferns. It felt good being with Chad, and for the first time in days nothing was worrying her.

Then Chad stopped dead, his face a little pale. "Hold back," he said softly.

"What's wrong?" asked Brittany in alarm.

"I don't think that Buttons ran away," he replied. "Or that he was run over, either."

"What do you mean?" Brittany pushed at his restraining arm to check out what he had seen.

She felt sick. The poor old cat was definitely Buttons. The calico fur made that clear. But someone or something had made it impossible to tell any other way. The cat had been literally ripped apart. There were long gashes in its body, and tattered pieces of internal organs scattered over the ground. Most had been pecked at by birds or animals, but it seemed that Buttons had died by being torn into pieces. Brittany had to work hard to prevent herself from throwing up.

"Who could have done this?" she asked, appalled.

"Your cousin comes to mind," muttered Chad, obviously nauseated by the sight, too. "There's nothing we can do here, though. Let's see if we can find Jeff." Taking her arm gently, he led her away from Buttons's remains.

Could Curtis have killed his own cat? Brittany had never liked her cousin, but she wouldn't have thought him capable of such savage cruelty. On the other hand, after what she'd witnessed at the cat show, she was no longer sure. Her head was spinning slightly with all her conflicting, confusing thoughts.

The pathway they followed led into the trees in the direction of her aunt's house. "Are you sure we're going in the right direction?" she asked Chad.

"No," he admitted. "But Jeff's car was parked beside this path, so it's logical to check it out. And—" Abruptly he stopped again. There was a frown on his face, and he gestured ahead of them into a small clump of trees on a slight hill.

Beyond the trees she could make out a chain-link fence and some familiar backyard toys. They were right behind her cousin's house, and anyone wanting a good look without being seen could get one from here. Then she saw what had caught Chad's eye. There was someone stretched out between the trees. A man, on his stomach, obviously observing the house.

"That's Jeff," Chad said softly. "He must have been trailing Curtis. We'd better be quiet."

Treading carefully, they made their way toward the other reporter. He didn't move or indicate in any way that he'd heard them approaching. Chad's frown deepened. When they were only a dozen or so feet away, Chad gave a cry and then sprang forward.

Brittany's heart started to race as she watched Chad grab Jeff Chaney's shoulder and shake it.

As the older man was rolled over, Brittany saw that his face was twisted in a mask of frozen terror. His body was stiff, and there were two small puncture holes in his neck.

CHAPTER

12

～～～

The following morning at school Brittany found Kay waiting for her. Brittany couldn't forget her last conversation with Kay, and she was tempted to blow her off. But when she saw Kay's eyes, she couldn't bring herself to do it. It was obvious that Kay was upset and had been crying.

"I'm sorry, Brit," the redheaded girl said, sounding sincere. "I was way out of line when I called you. I didn't mean to sound so . . ." She sighed. "When I open my mouth, the words tumble out without conscious thought."

Brittany knew she was probably being stupid, but she couldn't stay mad at Kay. It hurt her more than it hurt Kay, probably. "Let's forget it," she said. Then she poked a finger under Kay's nose. "But if you make one more crack about Chad, or flirt with him one teeny little bit, I swear—"

"I won't!" Kay said quickly. "Cross my heart and all the rest." She cheered up immediately. "Maybe we could even double sometime?" she suggested.

Brittany stared at her. "You're going with someone already?"

"No," Kay confessed. "But—hey, it's just a matter of time, right? Two, maybe three days tops."

She was probably right about that, too. Honestly, there didn't seem to be much that stopped Kay for long.

It was a dull day in some ways, but Brittany was glad for it. She'd had enough excitement the past week to last her a lifetime. Maybe even two lifetimes. And the day before had been almost too much. There had been another session with the police to explain finding Jeff Chaney's body, and then she had to tell her aunt about Buttons. Brittany had begun to feel as though she were living in a never-ending nightmare. A simple day of school was what she needed to relax her shredded nerves.

She saw Curtis twice, but he hurried away from her before she could talk to him. He was wearing a long-sleeved shirt, so she couldn't tell if he had scratches on his arm. Still, Brittany knew he'd be staying after school for weight-lifting practice. He'd have his shirt off then. She could wander into the gym and clear up at least one mystery.

As soon as the day was over, Brittany took off for the gym. Kay had ducked off somewhere, which was marvelous. It saved Brittany thinking up an excuse to get rid of her. She wasn't sure why, but she felt that having Kay around while she checked out Curtis would be a mistake.

On the way down the corridor to the gym, she ran into Donna Bryce. She hadn't spoken to the girl since their encounter in front of the school the previous week. The blond girl gave her a silent, icy stare and stormed into the girls' locker room.

Brittany moved down to the gym door and peered inside. There were a couple of boys in practice clothes. Talking to one of them was Kay. Brittany couldn't help smiling. So *that* was where Kay had disappeared to! She was lining up a date, maybe to double with her and Chad.

To her surprise, Chad walked up to her just then, a wide grin on his face.

"Hiya, gorgeous!" He gave her a soft peck on the cheek. "What are you doing here?"

"Believe it or not," she told him happily, "thinking about you. And checking up on Curtis," she admitted. "It's about time for him to work out."

Chad raised an eyebrow.

"Trying to find cat scratches," she replied to the question in his eyes.

"Smart thinking," he said. "And I'm here for much the same reason." He shifted uncertainly from foot to foot. "Look, I'll just be a moment, okay?" Without waiting for a reply, he slipped into the boys' locker room.

With no idea what he was doing, Brittany simply stayed in the corridor and waited. A moment later the door to the gym opened, and Kay came out.

"Here to check out the bods?" she asked, grinning.

"That's your job, not mine."

"True," agreed Kay, shivering happily. "I think Martin Tobey is going to ask me out tomorrow." Her eyes narrowed. "At least, he'd *better,* if he knows what's good for him."

Brittany smiled. The same old Kay.

"Well," her friend said, "I've got to go. I'll call you later." With a wave she swept out the outside door. As she did so, Curtis pushed his way in. Brittany heard Kay snap, "Well, *excuse* me!" Curtis slammed the door behind him without replying.

He was clearly in a bad mood, a heavy scowl on his face. Brittany saw that there was also a tic in his cheek, making him look as if he were blinking constantly. He was nervous, as well as angry—but about what?

As soon as he saw Brittany, Curtis stopped dead. His expression shifted from anger to guilt to worry and then back to anger. "Are you checking up on me?" he growled.

"Yes," Brittany answered, catching him off guard

with her honest answer. "Curtis, your mother is worried sick about you."

"That's her job," he replied. "So butt out." He started to move past her, raising his arm to push in the locker room door. Brittany gave a start when she noticed that his sleeves were rolled up.

There wasn't a mark on his arm. . . .

She grabbed his wrist. "What happened?" she demanded.

He jerked his arm away. "What are you talking about?" he mumbled, trying to act innocent, but Brittany had seen the fear in his eyes.

"I saw that cat claw several long gashes in your arm yesterday," she told him. "And then it bit you and ripped your flesh. But there's no sign of any injury there now."

"You must have made a mistake," he said, refusing to lift his eyes to look at hers.

"I haven't," she said slowly. "But somebody has. Curtis, what are you doing? How did you recover so quickly?"

"You're crazy," he snapped, trying to brush past her.

"No, I am not!" she growled back. "I know what I saw. And—another thing. How did you manage to suddenly get so good at weight lifting? You've beaten Grant's records. You're taking steroids, aren't you? The same ones that Grant took."

"Leave me alone!" he yelled, his face contorted with rage. "Get off my back! And if you say anything about this to anyone, I swear I'll kill you!"

"Like you killed Grant?" Brittany shot back.

Curtis shook his head vehemently. "I didn't kill him!"

"And Buttons?" she persisted. He glowered at that accusation and didn't even try to deny it. An inspiration seized Brittany. "Where'd you get that hickey?" she asked.

His hand flew up to his neck—the exact spot where Grant's wounds had been. Then he glowered at her and removed his hand slowly. "There's no—"

"No, there isn't," she agreed. "But you thought there might be, for just a second. Or else why would you try to cover it? Is that the spot where the steroids are injected?"

"I'm telling you one last time," Curtis growled, "back off. And shut that big mouth of yours. Otherwise you'll get hurt." He shoved her with the palm of his hand. Caught off guard, Brittany staggered back, as Curtis pushed on into the locker room.

As she caught her breath, she heard Curtis yell out inside the room, "Hey! What the hell do you think you're doing?" Then there was the sound of a scuffle, and the door flew open again. This time Chad tumbled out, followed by Curtis.

Her cousin was clearly furious now. The veins on his neck were bulging, and his fists were clenched. "You dirty little thief!" he howled, advancing on Chad.

Brittany saw with shock and concern that there was blood trickling out of the corner of Chad's mouth. He wiped at it with the back of his hand as he straightened up. She stepped between them, terrified that Curtis was going to punch Chad a second time. "Stop it!"

Curtis glared at her again. "So this jerk's with you?" he snarled. "It figures. Well, if I catch him rifling my locker again, I'm going to break his stupid neck." With that he whirled around and pushed back into the locker room.

"Now I know why I'm so honest," Chad said. "I'd make a lousy thief."

Brittany whirled around, ready to bawl him out for his stupidity. The sheepish look on Chad's face and the still-trickling blood stopped her protests. "You poor thing," she said sympathetically. After fishing a tissue from her shoulder bag, she crossed to him. Carefully she dabbed the blood away. "Does it hurt?" she asked.

"Will you kiss it and make it better if it does?"

"I'll kiss it anyway," she promised, and did so.

Chad hummed happily. "Then I'll be honest. Yes, it hurts. Almost as much as my ego. I can't believe I let myself get caught."

"What were you doing in his locker?" she asked.

"Looking for clues," Chad replied. "I figured it would be a good place to stash his steroids. But there was nothing in there that shouldn't have been."

"Why didn't you tell me what you were doing?" she asked. "I could have kept him out here and saved you a punch in the face."

He kissed her again. "If I'd done that, I'd have made you an accessory to the crime of breaking and entering. I like you just the way you are: innocent and cute."

"Flatterer."

"I work hard at it," he agreed. "So, what did you . . ." His voice trailed off to silence, and he stood staring at the ceiling. "I feel . . ." He didn't finish. He didn't have to.

The air thickened around Brittany, chilling her. A trickle of cold sweat crept down the small of her back. Her skin had turned icy, goose bumps springing up over every inch of her skin. Even her hair seemed to quiver with the terror that filled her body.

It was exactly how she had felt right before Grant had died!

She couldn't move. No matter how hard she struggled, it was impossible to move a muscle. She had to fight just to breathe.

Chad was rooted to the spot beside her, drops of sweat on his forehead, his skin so pale he looked almost dead. His eyes were fixed and staring, and she could see his muscles quiver as he struggled against the paralysis that held them both.

Again, there came the feeling of inhuman eyes focusing on her. As if something had crawled out of the deepest, darkest pit of hell to leave its footprints on her soul.

Then it was gone as suddenly as it had come. She almost collapsed from the relief of it. Chad grabbed her arms and she shivered at the coldness of his touch.

"That was it!" she gasped, her teeth chattering. "The same as when Grant was murdered!"

"It wasn't your imagination," Chad said. "I felt it, too." He stared at the locker room door. "Curtis!"

As he said the name, there came a howl of utter terror and total despair from within the locker room.

This time Brittany didn't hesitate a second. She slammed through the door one step ahead of Chad. There was a shiver of movement up by the window. It was gone before she could focus on it.

A strangled cry escaped from Brittany as she stared down at the floor. Curtis lay on his back, his chest unnaturally high. His expression was one of horror, and his skin was pale and drawn tightly across his bones.

On his neck was a wound exactly like the ones that had been on Grant's and Chaney's bodies: a red swelling of the jugular vein with two puncture marks.

CHAPTER
13

It took all of Brittany's willpower not to scream. She simply stared down at her cousin's body and felt the horror rise within her.

Chad hopped up onto a bench to stare out the window. When he then turned back to Brittany, he looked ready to throw up. "No sign of anyone," he muttered, obviously fighting to keep control.

In a repeat of the last time the locker room door was flung open and the coach stormed in. It took him a few seconds to focus. By then Miss Yates had run into the room, also.

"What . . ." the coach began, then shook his head. "Out—now!" Seeing Miss Yates, he threw out an arm. "Tammy, call the police. Now!"

Miss Yates swallowed as she caught sight of the corpse, then nodded and dashed from the room. Brittany wondered if she'd call the police before or after she threw up. Her own stomach was none too steady, and her head was whirling. Chad's arms were around her shoulders, and she was glad for his support and strength.

"Come on," he said quietly. "We'd better wait outside."

She wasn't going to argue. Staying with Curtis's corpse was not something she wanted to do. Besides, now that her mind was starting to work again, she had to make a phone call and fast.

As they left the locker room, Brittany saw Donna standing in the entrance to the girls' locker room. It was a rerun of the last murder! There was Donna, in a leotard, her hair messed up, and a light coating of sweat across her face and chest. Her eyes were bright, and she glared wordlessly at Brittany before moving back inside and closing the door.

"Maybe you'd better sit down," Chad suggested. "I know I want to."

"Not yet," she replied. "I've got to make a call." She shook off his hands and took several deep breaths. The spinning in her head had started to slow, but she knew she was still on the verge of freaking out. With care, she walked to the coach's office to find a phone there.

As Brittany, followed by a puzzled Chad, arrived, Miss Yates was replacing the receiver. She bolted past them and out the door, hand over her mouth. Brittany dialed the zoo, the direct line to her mother.

There was no answer. Odd. Surely Mom was still there, or at least Christina? After a moment she gave up, and dialed her mom's department number. A secretary answered.

"This is Brittany Harlow," she said. "Is my mother there? Dr. Harlow?"

"I'm afraid not," the secretary replied. "She left a short while ago. Her assistant is gone for the day as well."

"Thanks." Brittany replaced the receiver, then looked up at Chad. "That's odd."

"Yeah?" Chad shrugged. "Well, we've got worse things to worry about. Like another corpse, and the two of us once again being first on the scene. Why did you call your mother, anyway?"

"I figured she might be able to help if she took a fresh sample of Curtis's blood," Brittany explained. "And . . ." She stared at Chad. "This is going to sound like I've really lost it, but I also wanted her to take samples from the window."

"Samples?" Chad definitely looked puzzled. "Of what?"

"I'm not sure," Brittany admitted. "But . . . well, whcn we went in, I caught a glimpse of something disappearing through the window. It looked . . ."

Well, it didn't matter if he thought she was crazy; she *had* to say it. "It looked like a snake of some kind. A *very* large snake."

"Good." Seeing her confused expression, he added, "That's what I thought I saw. I was ready to believe *I'd* gone nuts. Especially since there was no sign of anything when I looked out the window."

"I wish I could say it made me feel better to know you saw it, too," Brittany admitted. "But I don't. I feel *terrible.*" All of the fear and shock and loss welled up inside her in an instant. She couldn't help it; even if she hadn't been on the best terms with Curtis, he had been her cousin. Tears clouded her vision, and then she was crying in great, heaving sobs.

Chad hugged her and she collapsed against his shoulder. Her crying wouldn't stop, and she could feel the tension in his body, too. He was just holding on to his emotions.

After a few minutes Chad murmured softly, "I think you'd better change shoulders; that one's soaked."

Brittany swallowed hard and straightened up. "I'm sorry," she gasped, fighting to stop crying. He handed her a tissue. Taking off her glasses with one hand, she wiped her eyes with the tissue in the other.

"Don't be," he replied. "You needed that cry."

She sniffed and nodded. "Yeah." She blew her nose and then replaced her glasses. They were streaked with her tears. "Now what?"

"Now we wait for the police," said Chad grimly.

* * *

Sergeant Kahn didn't appear to be any happier to see Brittany than Brittany was to see her again. With a sigh Kahn gestured for Brittany to sit down in the same classroom as last time. As before, Sergeant Jellicoe took up his position behind her.

"So this is the second body you and Chad Curran have found in two days," Kahn said, eyes focused on Brittany's face. "And your third in one week."

This wasn't going to be easy. Brittany knew it looked bad for her. She went red. "What do you mean?" she snapped.

"Why was Curran with you both times?" Jellicoe asked. "Did you know you'd need an alibi?"

"I didn't know Chad would be here today," Brittany replied. "And neither of us knew that Curtis was in danger."

"So." Kahn made a note on her pad. "Well, tell us what happened." She listened until Brittany was finished. Then she sighed. "It all sounds rather . . . far-fetched," she remarked.

"I can't help what it sounds like," Brittany replied, angry that the woman wouldn't believe her. "I'm just telling you what I saw."

"Your mother," put in Jellicoe, "told us there aren't any snakes as large as the one you claimed to have seen this time."

"I told you, I only *think* it was a snake I saw. It was moving fast, and I caught just a glimpse of it."

"All right," Sergeant Kahn said. "Let's leave the snake for the moment. Why were you outside the locker room this time?"

Brittany swallowed. She hadn't mentioned her suspicions, but she knew that she had no choice. "I had a feeling that Curtis was on steroids," she admitted. "I wanted to talk with him and ask."

Kahn raised an eyebrow. "And did he admit he was?"

"No. He just got angry with me."

"Not surprising," the woman replied. "If he *was* taking them, he'd hardly say so. And if he *wasn't,* he'd be furious." She seemed to be weighing something before she added, "We can't be *certain,* of course, until the autopsy, but I'm pretty sure you're right." Seeing Brittany's startled look, the sergeant smiled slightly. "We in the police aren't all morons, you know. We were keeping an eye on Curtis, to try to see who he might be getting his stuff from."

"He saw an awful lot of you, didn't he?" asked Jellicoe, over her shoulder.

"We're *cousins,"* Brittany snapped, realizing what the two of them were implying.

"True," Kahn agreed. "But you also have access to chemicals from your mother's well-equipped laboratory. One that you and your friend Kay visit a lot. One that stores snake venom. And one of two dead boys is your cousin. The other was the estranged boyfriend of your friend Kay. *Your* boyfriend—whose partner was murdered yesterday—is your only alibi for two of the killings. And this dead boy was the only other witness to the first murder."

133

Brittany could hardly believe what she was hearing. She didn't know whether she was going to be arrested or what. "What are you saying?" she demanded.

"Saying?" Sergeant Kahn shrugged her shoulders. "We're just trying to tell you how things appear to us. Maybe you could help clear some of it up? By the way, where's your friend Kay Johnson?"

Brittany hesitated and then answered, "I don't know."

"Lucky she wasn't around this time, isn't it?" said Jellicoe.

Did they know? Feeling that she might be betraying her friend, Brittany nevertheless said, "She *was* here. She left the building just as Curtis arrived."

"Really?" Kahn's eyes lit up with anticipation. There was no mistaking the predatory gleam in them this time. The woman smiled, the grin of a crocodile about to munch on lunch. "But you didn't see her reenter?"

"No."

Sergeant Kahn made another note. "I think I'd better have a little chat with Miss Johnson," she remarked.

"You think *she* killed Curtis?" Brittany asked. "But . . . why would she? And she wasn't connected to Jeff Chaney at all."

Kahn shrugged. "I haven't worked it all out yet," she said frankly. "But she *did* have a motive for murdering Witney. And she was in the vicinity when Curtis was killed. And we don't know where she was yesterday when Chaney was murdered. That's one of the things I want to ask her."

Brittany stared at the policewoman, aghast. Kahn clearly *wanted* Kay to be guilty. It would be a nice cut-and-dry case, then. Grant killed out of anger, Curtis and Jeff Chaney—well, Kahn would think of some reason. Maybe Curtis had lied to protect Kay, and Kay killed him because he was getting too much attention. Maybe Jeff because he'd found out something while he was snooping around. She wondered just how far the sergeant would go to nail Kay. Far enough to ignore other leads and suspects?

Then she remembered that Kay had admitted going out with Curtis once. *Both* of the teens murdered had dated Kay. Brittany realized that if Sergeant Kahn knew that, Kay could be in jail inside the hour.

"I guess you can go for now," Sergeant Kahn said, interrupting Brittany's thoughts. "I'll contact you later." To Jellicoe, she added, "I'll see Curran next."

Her head in a whirl, Brittany walked to the classroom door, where she saw Chad waiting. He gave her a quick hug.

"I'll call you later," he promised. "Be brave!" He went with Jellicoe into the room and the door closed.

Be brave? She wished she could! Her cousin was dead, and her best friend was the prime suspect. She found herself wondering if Kay could be guilty.

Kay was a lot of things—spoiled, inconsiderate, angry, and sometimes incredibly dumb. But Brittany couldn't believe that she was a killer. At the same time, though, she couldn't quite bring herself to reject the idea completely.

What to do? She decided to try calling her mom at home. Had she gotten sick and gone home early? She went to one of the phones in the hallway and dialed her home number. It rang several times without a reply. She was starting to get really worried and was about to hang up when there was a click, and her mother said sleepily, "Hello?"

"Mom!" Brittany exclaimed, relieved. "You're home!"

"Oh, hi, sweetheart. Yes, I'm home. And you're not. What's happened?"

Her heart sank as she realized what she had to do. "Mom, I've got terrible news. Curtis was murdered. He's dead, just like Grant."

"Dead?" It was only a squeak. "Oh, my God! Are *you* okay?"

"I'm okay," she replied.

"Right." Her mom was wide awake now. "I'll call Helen, to see what I can do. Then I'll be there to get you. Stay there."

Remembering her earlier idea, Brittany cut in quickly. "You'd better bring something to take a blood sample."

"Oh, yes. Good thinking. I'll be there soon." There was a click and the phone *burred* softly.

Brittany replaced the receiver. She walked back to the empty classroom to wait. She wished she could believe that things would get better, but she couldn't. How had Aunt Helen taken it when she learned that her son had been murdered? Dumb question, Brittany realized. She'd be heartbroken and might never recover.

Collapsing into a chair, Brittany sat numbly, staring off into space, weary and emotionally drained.

CHAPTER
14

~~~

By the time that Brittany's mother had taken blood samples, Brittany was on the verge of freaking out. It was too much. All the fear, and horror, and uncertainty were chipping away at her strength and mental stability. She felt as if the world around her was mad and she was adrift in it.

But at least Chad had shared the experiences with her. She felt better knowing he could at least corroborate her bizarre tales. The strange feelings of paralysis and dread, for example. And the half-sighting of a monstrous snake.

Once they were safe at home, her mother made them both mugs of steaming hot chocolate, and Brittany gratefully sipped at hers. "How are Aunt Helen and Uncle Joe?"

"Not good." Her mother sighed. "Helen's in a real state and had to be given tranquilizers. Joe's in shock, of course, but he's going to have to get it together for the arrangements.

"Arrangements?"

"You know—the burial. There's going to be an autopsy tomorrow. I've spoken with Dr. Vitelli, but it's pretty obvious that Curtis was killed by an injection of venom, just like the Witney boy."

"Mom, Chad and I both saw something. It *looked* like a huge snake, slipping out the locker room window. There definitely wasn't anyone in the locker room this time. We ran in right after we heard Curtis scream." She choked back a sob at the memory.

"A *snake?*" Her mom stared at her. "Sweetheart, you *know* there isn't a snake capable of killing a person like that."

"Yeah, that's what makes it worse. I saw something that I know couldn't exist." She hesitated, wondering if she should say what was on her mind. She decided she had no choice. "And I felt that coldness and the paralysis again. Just like the other night in my room, when I was sure something was with me."

"What do you mean?" her mother asked sharply.

"I think that whatever killed Grant, Curtis, and Jeff

139

Chaney was in my room that night," Brittany said slowly as her own thoughts came together. "I think I was *very* lucky that you came in when you did. It must have been after me."

"God, no!" Her mom grabbed her arm. "Why?"

"Because I sensed something that first time," Brittany replied. "I got the impression of something very evil and very *intelligent*. And maybe, somehow, it sensed me and thought I could cause trouble. I don't know. I'm just guessing."

After a few moments' silence her mother said, "If you're right, then it's bound to come after you again. Isn't it?"

Brittany nodded. "That's what scares me," she admitted. "I really do think it's going to try to get me again."

"Then you're sleeping in my room with me until this is over, one way or another," her mom said firmly. "I won't let anything happen to you. But . . ." She shook her head. "This is crazy. You *can't* have seen a giant snake. There's no such creature."

"I know that," Brittany agreed. "But I *did* see something."

"I believe you," her mother replied. "But I just wish we knew what it was."

"So do I!"

Chad called about an hour later. Brittany told him her theory about the snake killer going after the two of them next.

"It's a thought," he admitted glumly. "Maybe I should come and stay at your house for a few days."

"Why? So whoever it is can get us both together?"

"No, you idiot—so I can be there to help."

"Thanks for the offer, but I know my mom would never agree. And you're in just as much danger as I am."

"I don't think so," he replied. "I think that whoever is behind this snake business must know you. How else could they have found you so easily? It *has* to be someone you know at school or somewhere. Which means I'm probably a lot safer than you are. Whoever it is must think you know something that you don't."

"Like who the killer is, you mean?"

"Right."

"But I *don't* know," she objected. "If I did, he'd be in jail by now."

"You and I know that," Chad pointed out. "But the killer may not. The killer may *think* you know who he or she is, but that the police simply don't believe you yet. Maybe you even know some vital clue, but haven't recognized it for what it's worth, and the killer is afraid that you will sometime."

"I'm getting more and more confused by the minute," Brittany admitted.

"I don't mind your being confused," he replied. "I just don't want you getting dead. Be very careful, Brittany. I'm very fond of you. Do you have *any* idea who might be behind this?"

"I wish I did," she said.

"If this were a mystery novel," Chad said, "the killer would be the last person you'd suspect. So who would *that* be?"

"You," she told him.

He managed a chuckle at that. "Okay, maybe the second-to-last person you'd suspect. Just set your brilliant little mind to it and see if you can figure anything out. Good night."

Brittany, to her surprise, found herself getting quite tired. She imagined it was shock and strain taking their toll. Even with the threat that she might be the target of a killer hanging over her head, she couldn't stay awake. Too much had happened, and she was utterly drained. In the large, soft, warm bed she soon drifted off to sleep.

She awoke, thrashing about, held in a steel-tight grip. Gasping and choking, she struggled to escape from the hold. It was several seconds before she realized that it was her mother holding her, not some serpentine slayer. Her heart was hammering away, and her mind flooded with terrible images. Gradually she managed to get a grip on her terror and slowly calmed down.

"Brittany!" her mother gasped, looking pale in the dim light of the bedroom. "Are you okay? I was scared for a moment there."

"You were scared?" Brittany shuddered, managing to collect her thoughts. "It was just a dream. But a horrible one." She strove to recapture the vivid images that had disturbed her. "All disjointed, but so *real*. I remember Dad was in it, falling out of the sky, into the mouth of a snake. And the snake turned into an airplane, I think. All gleaming metal, and huge jet

engines. And I was being sucked into the engines, and I could see these metal blades inside that would cut me to shreds—" She was shaking just thinking about the nightmare. "Then it changed into a snake, but it had human eyes. And I knew that it was someone familiar to me. Only I couldn't quite see who it was. Then the snake lunged at me and bit me. It started to wrap around me, and I woke up."

"You were screaming," her mother told her. "Like you were trying to escape."

"I'm sorry I woke you, Mom."

Her mother smiled and stroked her hair. "That's okay, sweetheart. After the day you've had, I'm not surprised you had nightmares. Anyone would."

"It wasn't just a nightmare," Brittany said slowly. "It's like something I know subconsciously trying to come out in my dream. Only it was all twisted, and I couldn't get a hold of it."

"It all sounded terribly Freudian to me," said her mother. "You know, snakes and airplanes as symbols."

Brittany blushed. "It wasn't that kind of dream," she insisted. "The airplane is obvious; I'm still scared about losing someone close to me, and I think that someone is Chad. And the snake—" She shook her head. "It stands for somebody I know, I get that much. But that's all." She glanced at the clock. It was just after four A.M. "I'm never going to get back to sleep now," she said. "I think I'll make some coffee and read awhile before I get ready for school."

"All right, sweetheart." Her mother settled back down. "I, on the other hand, need all the rest I can get. With you gone, it should be a lot easier."

Brittany smiled slightly as she climbed out of bed. She headed for the kitchen and started a pot of coffee. While it bubbled away, she decided to look for something to read. None of the magazines really interested her. They seemed so frivolous. Instead, she went into the den where she had a small computer and her books crammed everywhere. There were some of her mother's here, too. She wanted something easy to read. Maybe she was awake, but she wasn't up to concentrating. She was sure she'd put a couple of trashy romance stories in there somewhere.

As she hunted, a thin hardcover caught her eye. There was a snake curling down the title on the spine. She was about to dismiss it as one of her mother's texts when she saw the title: *Goodness Snakes!* It certainly didn't sound like a textbook of any kind.

Brittany pulled it out and studied the cover. It was by some guy named William vande Water, whoever he was. The front cover illustration showed a pair of snakes wrapped around a stick. There was a technical term for the drawing, she knew—*caduceus,* that was it! Under the author's name was written: "Our love/hate relationship with snakes through the ages."

Well, it sounded interesting. Not too thick, and with a silly title like that it probably wasn't dull. Just the sort of thing to read with her coffee.

It turned out to be utterly fascinating. This vande Water had a bizarre sense of humor that made the book very readable. Starting with the story of the serpent in the Garden of Eden, he continued telling legends associated with snakes throughout the ages. One that was really fascinating was from the *Epic of Gilgamesh*. This was the oldest book in the world, dating back to before 3,000 B.C.

Gilgamesh was a king who had set off looking for immortality after the death of a friend. He found the plant that would make him immortal, but while the exhausted Gilgamesh slept, a snake had stolen and eaten the plant. This was why men die, the legend claimed, and why snakes can renew themselves by shedding their skins to become young once more.

This was nothing more than a story, she understood, but it showed something of the fascination some people had with snakes. They were sometimes a symbol for evil and sometimes a symbol for healing.

Healing . . .

The memory of Curtis being mauled by the cat at the show came back to her mind. Yet, when she looked at his arm the next day, it had been completely healed. . . .

She stared at the book, hardly daring to think. What if there was something in this healing effect of snakes? Weren't a lot of pharmaceutical drugs derived from plants? Would it be completely amazing if there was one that could be gotten from a reptile?

That steroidlike stuff in Grant's blood—could it have been from a snake? Some weird substance that built up a person's body? Made him stronger, better, and healthier?

Brittany was half-convinced that her mind was still partially dozing. These were the sort of thoughts that came to you in dreams. The kind of logic that seems perfectly reasonable when you're asleep, but falls apart completely when you wake up.

On the other hand . . .

Go with it, she told herself. As Sherlock Holmes said, "When you have eliminated the impossible, whatever is left—however improbable—must be the truth." Okay, so try out the theory. Some kind of snake-derived drug that acts like a steroid. Accepting that, the next question had to be: Who could have made such a thing?

The obvious answer was—Mom.

Brittany didn't even want to think of her as a possibility. Aside from everything else, she simply *knew* her mother was incapable of hurting anyone. She'd never even whomped Brittany's behind, despite the fact that Brittany knew she'd been bratty at times. The thought that she might be a killer was simply absurd.

Rule her out, then. What about Christina? Mom always said she was a capable assistant, and pretty smart. And she did study snakes. But did she have enough smarts to discover, process, and reproduce a drug that was light-years ahead of anything that anyone else on earth had ever managed? It didn't seem likely, but maybe not impossible.

Okay, leave her as a suspect. Who else?

The other people who were possible suspects in the killings looked even less like they could have produced a wonder drug. Kay? She couldn't even make chicken soup! Donna? She showed absolutely no interest in school at all. The coach? Or Miss Yates? Brittany doubted that either of them was smart enough to make such a drug.

But either of them might know where to buy it.

Brittany gave it up with a yawn. She was getting nowhere. She stopped trying to think things through and went back to her book.

She was so fascinated with it that she took it to school with her the next day. A feeling that she was getting somewhere was strong, even if she had no visible progress.

Kay was waiting for her at school. Her friend looked as if she hadn't slept, and her eyes were almost the same color as her hair.

"I wish I could think of a positive way to say this," Brittany told her, "but you look terrible."

"I know." Kay *had* to be feeling down to let an insult like that past her. "I was up half the night with that lousy Sergeant Kahn. She dragged me in to question me late in the evening." Then she gave a start. "Oh, Brit, I'm sorry! I should have—Damn. Curtis was killed yesterday after school, I'm sorry. How do *you* feel? It's selfish of me to think about what I'm going through right now."

Brittany was touched—and somewhat surprised—by Kay's concern. "I'll live," she replied. "And I'm afraid it was my fault that the police talked to you. I told them you'd been in the area when Curtis was killed. I figured that it was better than them finding out from someone else."

"It wasn't your fault," Kay said. "Apparently Donna spotted me, too, and demanded that they arrest me for murder. There's enough venom in her to kill me if I even look at her."

Brittany shivered. It was an unfortunate choice of words, considering some of the thoughts running through her own mind right then. Was Donna *really* convinced that Kay was guilty? Or was she just trying to cover up her own guilt? "I think that Sergeant Kahn is pretty convinced you're the killer," she admitted.

"Oh, don't I know it." Kay scowled. "Nothing I said to her made any difference. The only reason I'm not in jail right now is because she can't explain how I actually could have killed either Curtis or Grant. Or why I would have killed Jeff Chaney." Kay gave a heavy sigh. "Brittany—I *have* to ask. Do *you* think I'm guilty? That I killed them?"

I wish you hadn't asked me that! Brittany thought. She wished she could say no with a clear conscience. "I don't think you'd kill anyone," she said finally.

Kay grabbed her and hugged her tight. Brittany felt tears from Kay's cheeks on her own. "Thanks, Brit," she said. "I really needed to hear you say that." She released Brittany. "I know I'm not the best friend anyone could have." When Brittany opened her mouth to protest, Kay shook her head firmly. "Come on, Brit—be honest with me. I *know* I'm a pain sometimes. It's just that I can't help myself. I do stupid things without thinking. I could kick myself some days."

"Well, if you ever need someone to give you a swift kick . . ." Brittany said and grinned. "But you *are* my best friend, Kay, and part of being a friend is accepting that neither of you is perfect. And also that, despite everything, there's a bond between you."

"Thanks," said Kay. "I think." She managed a very watery smile. "Well, I guess it's time for another day of being educated."

"This," said Kay, "is a very weird book." It was outside during lunch, and Brittany had been showing her the *Goodness Snakes!* she'd been reading. "Did you see the bits about snake people? The Navajo believed that there were a whole race of them living beside a lake. Bizarro!"

"You think that's weird?" asked Brittany. "What about the Greek story of Cadmus? He killed a snake, then planted its teeth, and each one grew into an armed warrior. And the Vikings believed that an evil, giant snake would attack and help bring about the end of the world."

Kay gave her a strange look. "You don't sound like you think it's too weird."

Brittany squirmed slightly. "Well, I don't *believe* it," she said. "But . . . Both Chad and I saw what we thought was a huge snake slithering out the window of the boys' locker room. At the moment I'm willing to believe almost anything. But only almost."

"You obviously think there's something—well, abnormal about these murders."

Brittany spoke slowly. "I can't help it. Before both Grant's and Curtis's murders, I felt this—well, presence of something evil and intelligent. I was so shocked and terrified I couldn't move at all. Yesterday Chad felt it, too. Something powerful, lethal, and very, very inhuman. I don't know what it was."

"So you're hoping for answers in that book?" Kay asked. To Brittany's surprise, Kay wasn't making fun of her.

"I don't know." Brittany patted the volume. "There are a lot of cultures that have some kind of snake divinity as evil. Look at the Bible, for example. In the story of the Garden of Eden, the devil turns up as a serpent. The Aztecs believed in a giant winged serpent. The Egyptian pharaohs even wore a serpent head on their crowns as a symbol of power. I just don't know what to think right now, and I'm desperate enough to consider snake legends for an answer."

"Speaking of answers," said Chad's voice, "I've got a couple that might interest you."

Brittany whirled around, thrilled to see him. He had come upon them quietly and was standing several feet away, a notebook in hand. He grinned as Brittany hurried to greet him with a kiss.

"Mmmm," he murmured appreciatively. "I have to remember to surprise you more often."

"So why *did* you surprise us?" Brittany asked, drawing him back to where Kay was waiting, sitting under a tree.

"I was checking on some notes that Jeff had left and think that he may have found a new suspect. One that nobody else had thought of."

"Really?" Brittany felt a surge of hope. Maybe they could clear up the whole mystery and clear Kay!

"Really."

Kay tapped her foot loudly. "Are you going to tell us, or do I have to drag it out of you?"

Eyes sparkling, Chad said, "It's Miss Vale."

"Miss Vale?" Brittany had to recall who she was. "The school nurse?" She knew how skeptical she must sound.

"The school nurse," Chad agreed. "Jeff did a little research and discovered that ten years ago Miss Vale was Sarah Vale." He was met with blank faces. "Doesn't ring a bell? That's probably why the police haven't picked up on it yet. But Sarah Vale was an outstanding high school gymnast ready for the Olympic trials, but her whole career blew up when she was tested for drugs."

"Let me guess," Brittany said slowly, excitement mounting inside her. "She was on steroids!"

"You got it," he confirmed. "And at the times of both school murders, Nurse Vale was right here—in her office just a corridor away. Alone."

CHAPTER
15

‌

It made sense to Brittany. "If she had used steroids," she said slowly, "she might still know where to get them."

"And she doesn't have an alibi for the time of either school murder," said Chad triumphantly. "And nobody's asked her where she was when Jeff was killed."

"I'd like more than anyone for the killer to be proven to be anyone but me," Kay said. "But you don't have any proof. Just a theory. A nice theory, but so is Brittany's flaky supernatural idea. Unless you can get something substantial, it's just a theory."

"Kay—" Brittany said, annoyed at her friend.

"No," Chad said unexpectedly. "Kay's right. All I've got is a theory. Thanks, Kay. Sometimes I get too carried away with my own brilliance. You've got more brains than I have, obviously."

Kay seemed startled by this response. "Nobody's ever accused me of having brains before."

"Don't get used to it," Brittany said, a shade angrier than she'd intended.

"Well," said Chad, "I guess I'd better see if I can stir things up a little."

"How?" asked Brittany, suddenly concerned for him.

"The obvious answer is to let Miss Vale know what I know and then see what she says."

"That could be dangerous, if she *is* a drug dealer and killer," Brittany pointed out.

"Why don't we go with him?" Kay suggested. "That way she couldn't try anything. And if she does let something slip, we'd make good witnesses in court."

Chad gave her an admiring look. "I may have misjudged you, Kay," he told her. "You're doing some pretty swift thinking."

Jealousy stung Brittany. She hated herself for it, because she was certain that Chad was only being honest, but she couldn't help feeling that Kay was starting to get her claws into *her* boyfriend. She felt even more guilty a moment later.

"I'm just trying to protect Brittany," Kay replied.

"You're her first boyfriend, and I wouldn't want you to get murdered before she's ready to dump you. It might hurt her self-esteem."

"Ummm . . . Before we all start weeping on one another's shoulders, maybe we'd better go see Miss Vale?" Chad appeared a trifle uncomfortable as he led the way into the building.

Brittany's mind was whirling. Kay was expressing concern for her in a way she never had before. Maybe she really *had* turned over a new leaf. Or . . . maybe she just wanted to *look* as if she had. If Kay were the killer, then she might just be trying to dampen Brittany's suspicions. She didn't want to think like that, but it refused to go away. If they could get Miss Vale to confess, it would solve a lot of problems.

Of course, confronting a possible killer wasn't exactly high up on her list of smart things to do. "Shouldn't we call the police?" she suggested nervously.

"And tell them what?" asked Chad. "As Kay said, we need something more than a theory. But I promise I'll call Sergeant Kahn the first chance I get and let her know what I think." They were at the nurse's office now. Taking a deep breath, Chad rapped on the door, opened it, and walked in.

Brittany had been to the nurse a couple of times over the past two years for minor problems, but she'd never really noticed her. Now, with Chad's suspicions uppermost in her mind, she examined the young woman more carefully.

The nurse was in her late twenties, and very attractive. Her slim body showed signs of her athletic background, and her long blond hair was caught up in a ponytail. Her eyes were pale and blue, and she was clearly a professional. "Yes? Is one of you having a problem?"

"Kind of," Chad admitted. "You know about the two murders here in school?"

Miss Vale's eyes narrowed. "Everyone does. Why?"

Chad took a clipping from his wallet and held it out to her. "I found this in my newspaper's files," he said. "Sarah Vale, ten years ago."

Miss Vale stared down at the clipping and then back up at them. She shook her head. "That was a long time ago. I was young then," she replied coldly. "And I made a bad decision. I paid for it, so it's behind me now."

"Is it?" asked Chad carefully. "Both Curtis Harlow and Grant Witney were taking steroids, you know."

His meaning got through to Miss Vale all at once. Her face became red, and her eyes narrowed with anger. "Are you accusing *me* of providing them with drugs?"

"It's a thought," he replied.

"Well, you can stop thinking it," she snapped. "I told you it was behind me. I was stupid once; I wouldn't be stupid like that twice. I don't have anything to do with that stuff anymore."

"I'd like to believe it," Chad answered.

"No, you wouldn't," Miss Vale said. "You'd like to

think I was addicting two boys to steroids, wouldn't you? Well, I *wasn't*. And if a word about this leaves this room"—she glared at them all—"then I am going to sue the three of you for slander. Do I make myself clear?"

Chad was crestfallen as he picked up the clipping. With a shade of defiance in his voice he replied, "I have to tell the police about this, you know."

"Do you?" Miss Vale stared coldly at him. "Then you'd better tell them. And *only* them. Now get out—all of you."

Brittany was only too glad to leave. Chad and Kay seemed to agree. In the hall Chad leaned against the nearest wall and winced.

"Well, I deserved that, I guess," he said. "Prize chump, that's me."

"But she was *bound* to deny it," objected Brittany.

"Sure," agreed Chad. "But she's obviously not worried about our telling the cops. Just not anyone else. If she was guilty, the last people she'd want us to talk to would be the police. Therefore, she's probably innocent."

"Then you're giving up?" Brittany asked. "Maybe she realized that the best way to stop you talking was to act like she didn't mind."

"Maybe," he agreed. "I still plan to give Sergeant Kahn this clipping because I don't want her to accuse me of withholding information. But I really think I've made a fool of myself. I'd wager thousands that Sarah Vale has nothing to do with this."

"Great," said Kay. "That puts us right back where we started. With *me* as the prime suspect."

As they started to walk away from the office, Chad suddenly frowned. "Wait a second, Kay. Earlier, you said something about Brittany having a weird theory." He looked at both girls. "At the moment I'm feeling very stupid. I'm more than willing to admit that you can both think rings around me. So—what's this theory?"

Brittany blushed. "If I could think rings around you, I'd have stopped you from going through with that," she replied. "But I was hoping you'd stumbled across the right answer." She shrugged. "Well, mine isn't really a theory. It's just some odd ideas that haven't come together yet." She showed him the book *Goodness Snakes!* "There's a lot in here about snakes and our relationships with them. They're often a symbol of evil, but can also be a symbol of healing."

"So?"

"Well, Curtis had been on steroids, right? And we both saw him being clawed pretty badly by that cat at the show, but he healed impossibly fast from it. Could the two be connected? And connected with that paralysis we both felt?"

"I don't know," Chad admitted. "It sounds pretty thin to me." Brittany's hopes sank, and he sensed this. "Look, why don't we try to figure it out tonight? I'd love to come over and study that book with you."

"I've heard that line before," Kay broke in. "Study the book. Right!"

"You don't have to be so protective of me!" snapped Brittany. "I can look after myself—if I want to."

"Ex-cuuse me!" said Kay, obviously irritated.

"Peace!" shouted Chad, holding up his hands. "Kay, why don't you join us? You've been doing some reading, too, and you've been coming up with bright ideas."

Brittany felt annoyed and jealous for a moment. Then she realized that she was acting badly. Chad was right: Kay *was* being very helpful. Probably more so than she was. "Yes," she agreed. "Kay, please come," she said as the bell rang and the hall started to fill with students.

Surprised and pleased, Kay nodded. "Okay," she replied. "I'd love to."

The plans went haywire. When Brittany arrived home, there was no sign of her mother, but there was a message on the answering machine. She played it back and discovered that it was from her mother.

"Hi, Brittany," the recorded voice said. "Would you be a sweetheart and baby-sit Timmy and Jacquie tonight? Uncle Joe, Aunt Helen, and I have to make funeral arrangements for Curtis." The pain was strong in her mother's voice. "I'll be going directly to the funeral home from work, so eat something before you go over."

Just what she needed. Brittany liked her cousins, but they were a handful at the best of times. And this definitely was not the best of times. Still, there was no way she could get out of this gracefully. She called her aunt to let her know she'd be over shortly. She had no choice but to help. Then she called Chad and told him of the change in plans.

"No trouble," he said. "I'll just come over there instead. Have you called Kay yet?"

"She's next," Brittany answered.

"Okay," Chad said, "why don't I pick her up, and then we'll meet you at, oh, six-thirty?"

Chad and Kay alone together? Brittany felt her jealousy rising. But she forced herself to be rational. It was a nice gesture on Chad's part, and offering Kay a ride made sense. It was nothing more. "Sure," she agreed. "I'll let her know." Wishing she could be less suspicious, she phoned Kay to tell her the new plans.

"Okay," Kay agreed. A bit too readily? "I'll be waiting." Then she added, "Brittany, don't worry. I *promise* not to steal him or anything, okay?"

"Uh, I w-wasn't thinking—" Brittany stammered, flustered and embarrassed.

"Yes, you were," Kay replied. "And it's my fault. Brit, I meant what I said earlier, I'm sorry for my behavior. It was horribly cruel of me, and I promise not to repeat it. And I won't try to get between you and Chad."

Brittany believed her. "Thanks, Kay," she replied. "I needed to hear that, and I'm really glad you said it. It does reassure me a lot."

"Fine. See you later, agitator."

* * *

159

"When we get married," said Chad after Timmy and Jacquie were in bed, "we are *not* having kids." He collapsed onto the sofa beside Brittany and groaned.

Brittany's lips curled upward in a smile. "That's the worst proposal I've ever heard," she replied.

"Oh?" asked Kay. "And what was the best?"

"I'm still waiting for that," Brittany answered.

"I *thought* I was out of my skull for agreeing to play with those two fiends you call a nephew and a niece," Chad said. "But I *know* I'm totally nuts for competing with a female Laurel and Hardy team."

Brittany smiled fondly at him. "You're just a masochist, I guess," she told Chad.

"Probably," he agreed. "I'm still smarting from that confrontation with Miss Vale. So, what have you managed to gather from this book of yours?"

Brittany folded her legs beneath her and laid the book across her lap. "That there's a strong link through the ages between good and evil connected with snakes. Between healing and destruction."

"I did a bit of reading, too," Kay interrupted. "Don't look so surprised! I *can* read, you know. Anyway, did you know there's an old English myth about giant snakes? They were called wyrms—that's with a *y*, not an *o*. They lived underground and preyed on people. There are even some folks who think the Loch Ness Monster is some kind of immense snake."

Chad shrugged. "There have been reports of giant snakes going back forever," he agreed. "But they're no more than legends or people with one too many beers seeing things."

"What about what we saw in the locker room?" Brittany challenged. "I know *I* hadn't been drinking. Or thinking up legends."

"Yeah," Chad agreed. "That is kind of hard to explain. I mean, I only caught a glimpse of it, but it sure looked like a giant snake to me."

"And then there's Curtis's amazing healing," added Kay. "And we *know* he suddenly increased his strength and stamina, because Brittany and I both saw it. It has to be because of the steroids." She frowned. "I think we may be on to something with this snake angle, anyway, because I saw what looked like a hickey on his neck when he was working out that day. Right on his jugular."

Chad snorted. "What are we talking about here?" he asked. "A giant snake that bites people and gives them either super powers or kills them?"

"Maybe," said Brittany, not backing down. "It would explain why both Grant and Curtis had enough venom in them to kill a dozen elephants. If they had healing steroids in them already, maybe it would take that much venom to kill them."

"Whoa," said Chad. "Time out." He looked from Brittany to Kay. "What we're leading up to here is *way* over the edge into the Twilight Zone. You two are talking *intelligent* snake, aren't you? One that knows whether to kill or cure."

Brittany had to admit it had occurred to her.

"Not quite," Kay argued. "We're talking about an intelligence *guiding* the snake." She gestured at the book. "Someone who can make snakes do things they

wouldn't normally do. Some people have extraordi-
nary powers over animals. What if someone has
figured out a way to make this giant snake do what he
or she wants? Some form of ESP or hypnotism or
something?"

Chad considered the idea. "You mean that there's a
human being behind all this. You know, that's wild—
but it's not impossible."

"I'm with you there," Brittany agreed. The image of
someone sending out a giant snake to wreak havoc on
his or her foes was astounding, but maybe just plausi-
ble. "But who could it be?"

"Well, let's go over our clues," suggested Chad. "It's
got to be someone who knew all three victims, and
probably someone close by. I can't imagine that a
snake even like we're suggesting could travel far on its
own."

"Right," agreed Brittany. "We'd better leave Jeff
Chaney out of it for now, since we don't know exactly
what he was working on yet, or what led him to be
spying on Curtis." On a pad of paper she started to
write down names. "There was the coach and Miss
Yates. Donna. Kay and myself. Mom and Christina.
Those two boys in the gym when Grant was killed."

"And," added Kay, "there was Nurse Vale."

"Okay," Brittany agreed, adding her name to the
list. "Now, when Curtis was killed, there was the
coach and Miss Yates again. And Donna. Myself and
Kay. And Chad."

"But you and I were together," Chad pointed out.
"So we can alibi each other."

"But not me," said Kay glumly.

"It's not that simple," Brittany said reluctantly. "You see, if the killer was a snake sent by someone, then either Chad or I could have set it going."

"So we have to suspect ourselves, too," said Chad. "We aren't getting very far."

"Yes, we are," argued Kay. "We can rule out those two boys, and Christina and Brittany's mom?"

"No, we can't," said Brittany. "Neither Mom nor Christina was at work when Curtis was killed. Mom said she had a headache and had to go home to sleep. I don't know where Christina was, and those two boys could have slipped out of the gym. And Nurse Vale was supposedly in her office, but all alone. The list isn't any shorter at all."

"Okay," said Chad. "How about a different approach? The steroid in the blood. If that stuff *is* a wonder drug, wouldn't whoever controls the snake be on it, too? I mean, Grant and Curtis wouldn't be the only ones to have it, would they? He or she would be taking it, too."

"Right!" Brittany agreed. She felt excited that they might be on the right track now. "So whoever the killer is, he or she would be very healthy."

"Which rules you out," said Chad happily. "With your eyesight, you're obviously not the guilty person."

"But that doesn't narrow things down too much," Kay argued. "Let's face it, I'm pretty healthy, and so are you. In fact, everyone on that list is."

"Except my mom," said Brittany. "She's got some kind of blood disorder."

"Nothing serious?" asked Chad.

"She says not, but she's taking some kind of medication." Brittany gave a brittle laugh. "I never thought I'd appreciate it, but her being sick does mean she's innocent."

Chad shook his head. "We're not getting too far, are we? Let's face it, as detectives we'd be failures. We've got lots of leads, but nothing from any of them."

"I don't know," replied Brittany. "I can't help feeling that the answer's right here, in this book." She tapped the cover. "But I simply can't work it out."

"Whoever the killer is seems to think that you do have the answers," Kay said. "Which means you're probably in danger. You should make sure you are never alone for long."

"Okay," said Chad with a grin. "I volunteer to keep her company overnight."

"Pig," said Brittany, lightly punching his arm.

"Okay," he said, giving a mock groan. "How about just when you're taking showers?" He held up his hands before she could punch him again. "Hey, you can't blame me for trying."

"You're terrible," Brittany told him affectionately.

At that moment the front door opened. Uncle Joe walked in, looking tired and old. Aunt Helen and Dr. Harlow followed, both bedraggled and red-eyed. Brittany didn't need to ask how it had gone. She felt a great sense of loss over Curtis, and she hadn't really liked him. How must his parents be feeling? she asked herself.

"Time to go home," said Chad softly as the three of them stood up.

"Hi, sweetheart," said Dr. Harlow. "I'll be along shortly, okay?"

Brittany realized that her mother wanted to stay with her aunt and uncle for a while. "Sure, Mom."

"I'll stay with her till you come home, Dr. Harlow," Chad offered.

"We'll stay," said Kay firmly. Before Chad could say anything more, she added: "You have to drive me home, remember?"

"Oh. Right."

Brittany felt rather glad that Chad had actually forgotten. It was nice to see that she didn't have any real reason to be jealous of him and Kay. Incredible as it might seem, he really was interested in her.

Chad drove the couple of blocks back to Brittany's house in silence. Brittany was glad of that. She felt pretty subdued herself right then. It was really sad to see her relatives so broken up. When they reached her house, Chad parked the car and the three of them got out and started up the path together.

It was a dark, moonless night, the only light from the porch lamp, which Brittany had remembered to turn on before leaving earlier. Without warning, a chill whirled about them. Brittany shuddered, and Chad reached out to put his arm around her.

He never finished the gesture.

Brittany had removed her key and put it in the lock. She turned the key and opened the door when the full force of the chill enveloped her. Her throat went dry, and she felt her heart hammering inside her ribs. She managed to turn away from the door before she could no longer move a muscle.

She was paralyzed again as she had been before. And each time before, someone had died.

CHAPTER

16

Brittany was terrified. She couldn't move; even her eyes were frozen in their sockets. A clammy sweat had started to trickle down her back. Her heart pounded wildly, like that of a trapped animal. Which she was.

And so were Chad and Kay. Her friends stood, shaking slightly, their eyes wide. Both were pale, and it wasn't because of the low-level lighting. They had to be feeling the same wave of panic, nausea, and terror that had engulfed her.

There came a rustling sound in the large maple tree

on the front lawn. The branches seemed to shiver. There was a flash of metallic light, and Brittany stared, appalled, at the shape slowly slithering out of the tree.

There was no doubt about what she was seeing. It was an immense snake. Over fifteen feet long and eight or nine inches thick. Its head swayed slightly as the huge body twined down the trunk of the tree and slid to the ground. It was olive green with thin yellow stripes running from the head to the tail. As it touched the grass, the snake arched up and stared at the three of them. Its head was human in size, though not in shape. The long, thin snout probed toward its frozen victims. The eyes were yellow, slitted, and malevolent. The mouth opened, and the snake hissed softly. A long forked tongue flickered, and then withdrew.

Two large fangs were visible, moist and curved. Two fangs spaced like the marks on the three bodies she had seen.

Despite all of her theorizing, Brittany was stunned to see that there really was a gigantic snake. She knew that there had never been anything like it before in the animal kingdom. It was a huge, venomous serpent, filled with poison and malice.

Slowly it slithered across the grass toward the three of them.

Brittany struggled to overcome the paralysis that held her in place, but to no effect. But now she understood it—not that her understanding would help! Some snakes seemed to possess a power to mesmerize their prey. The victims would simply sit and wait till the serpent devoured them. This immense freak of nature obviously possessed the same hypnotic powers. Its mere presence caused the motor responses in its victims to freeze up. That must have been how the snake managed to kill Curtis and Grant. They had been frozen before the attack.

She, Chad, and Kay were doomed, then, and there was absolutely nothing that any of them could do. Any second now that terrible head would thrust forward and fasten those two, poison-tipped fangs into her neck. Or Kay's. Or Chad's. And then, in blazing agony, the venom would be injected.

They would be dead within a second.

The snake continued to slither slowly toward them. The two yellow eyes burned with an inner evil, focusing in hatred upon Brittany. As she met that dreadful gaze, Brittany recognized something. In a sudden rush of insight, she *knew*.

This was no creature controlled by someone else. This snake was *intelligent*. It was making its own decisions. No one was forcing it to act. What it did, it did from its own will. It was a snake the size of a person—with the intelligence of a person.

And the snake knew that she knew. Brittany could read the hatred in its eyes, and she could see that it recognized her as a foe. Hissing louder than before, it arched up, head thrust back to be ready for the downward plunge that would end with the two gleaming fangs buried in her jugular.

An intensely loud siren suddenly sliced through the night.

Abruptly the paralysis was broken, and Brittany could move again. As the snake recoiled in shock, Brittany flung herself against the door and threw it open. Chad grabbed Kay and hauled her inside. Brittany slammed the door and shot the safety bolt home.

The door shuddered as the snake slammed into it. It was probably hissing and screaming in fury at the loss of its prey, but nothing could be heard over the shriek of the alarm. The door shuddered a second time. Brittany screwed her eyes closed, leaning on the door as if to bolster it against the attack. But there were no more assaults.

"What is that noise?" Chad yelled in her ear. She could barely make out the words.

"The alarm!" she yelled back. "You have only thirty seconds to turn it off when you open the door; otherwise it sounds!"

"Thank God it did!" he howled. "It broke the snake's spell."

Brittany nodded. Chad had obviously reached the same conclusion she had. The sudden shock of the alarm had distracted the serpent, allowing them to escape. If she hadn't been paralyzed while opening the door, the three of them would be dead now.

The howling noise was annoying, but was it safe to turn it off? Or would the snake return? She doubted that the snake would try again that night. The alarm would have woken half the neighborhood by now. Desperate for silence, Brittany punched in her code number. The sudden silence made the ringing in her head echo even more.

Then the ringing was the phone. Chad scooped it up and answered it. "Um, it's the alarm company. They want a code word not to call the police."

"Oh." She managed to stir herself into action finally. Shaking, she took the phone. "It's Brittany Harlow," she said. "The alarm went off—um, while I was kissing my boyfriend. The codeword is *Father.*" The woman on the other end acknowledged, and Brittany replaced the receiver.

Then the shock of what had happened really hit her. She collapsed onto the sofa, shivering and gasping. Chad grabbed hold of her. His skin felt as cold as her own, and she could feel the tremors in his body. They clung to each other for several wordless seconds, seizing comfort from being close. Then Brittany remembered Kay.

Her friend was sitting on the floor, her arms wrapped tight about her knees, her face buried in her lap, shaking badly. With some reluctance Brittany broke Chad's grip and went over to Kay. Her eyes wide with terror, Kay just stared silently. Chad joined them, putting an arm around each girl. The three of them clung to one another as if their sanity depended upon it.

It probably did.

Eventually the panic died down to a bearable level. Brittany started to feel warmth returning to her fingers and toes. Her heart had slowed its frantic pace, and she felt as if she could talk without fainting. Pulling back from the group hug, she stared at Kay and Chad. The color was returning to their skin now.

"I guess that answered some of our questions," Brittany managed to say, despite her teeth chattering.

"Too damned many, if you ask me," Chad agreed.

"It was *real*," whispered Kay.

"We were right," Brittany said to Chad. "We had seen a giant snake."

"No!" exclaimed Kay firmly. "That was *not* a snake."

"What are you talking about?" asked Chad. "Didn't you see that sucker? It was a—"

"That was not a snake," Kay repeated. "It just *looked* like a snake. That was a *person*." She shuddered. "I stared into those eyes, and someone was in there staring right back at me."

"I think Kay's right," agreed Brittany. "That snake —or whatever it was—was definitely intelligent. I could *feel* the evil mind inside it. It hated us and was gladly going to murder the three of us. If the alarm hadn't gone off . . ." There was no need to say any more.

"It's all in that book," Kay said, seeing that Chad was still struggling to accept the idea. "Snake people, remember? The Navajo believed in them. The wyrms could change themselves into human beings. The Greeks believed in *lamias*—snakes that could become beautiful women. It's all there. And it's all true! We just saw one. It almost killed us!"

"I don't know," Chad finally said. "I mean . . . a

person who can change into a snake? That's way too Looney Tunes for me."

"But not for me," Brittany announced. "I agree with Kay. I could see past the eyes into the poisonous soul of that creature, and there was a person inside looking back at me. Only . . . only I couldn't make out who it was. But whoever it was knows us. That person knew we had an alarm system installed, and that if he or she wanted to kill us, it would have to be while we were outside. It just screwed up by waiting a few seconds too long." She glared at Chad. "I don't care if you think I'm crazy—that was definitely a person, not a snake."

Chad shook his head. "I told you, you're the most levelheaded and intelligent person I know. If you're so sure and Kay agrees with you, I'd have to be very stupid not to accept it. But *who* is it?"

"I don't know," Brittany admitted. "It's someone familiar, but . . ." She managed a weak grin. "Well, we know for certain that it isn't Kay."

"Thanks," said Kay. "But we're still the only ones who *are* convinced that I'm innocent. And I doubt that Sergeant Kahn will accept it if we tell her that the killer she's looking for is someone who can turn into a snake. I think we'd get locked up in a psych ward for life. Which would very severely cramp my social life, you know."

"We need some kind of proof," Chad agreed. "Until then, I think we'd better keep quiet about all this." He gave Brittany an apologetic look. "Even your mother, I'm afraid."

Brittany hated to keep anything from her mom, but she could see the logic to it. "Yeah. She might think we're all flaking out. And I wouldn't want her to split us up."

"Me, either," said Chad. "I've gotten kind of used to having you around."

Kay made gagging sounds. "I think I'll make a pit stop," she announced.

"Good idea," agreed Brittany. While Kay was gone, she and Chad comforted each other. It made her feel a great deal better and able to cope.

As Brittany got ready for school the next morning, she shivered. When would the snake person try again?

Kay met her at school. "Bummer of a night," she said. "I couldn't sleep. Brittany, I don't mind admitting it—I'm *scared.*"

"So am I," Brittany said. "We'd have to be megastupid *not* to be scared. But there's got to be something we can do. There's *got* to be."

If only she could think of it!

Getting through the day without screaming took all of her concentration. Donna Bryce was working on stirring the other students up against her and Kay, but Brittany didn't even care. Only one thought went through her mind as she glowered at Donna: *Is it you? Are you the snake?*

The memory of that serpent refused to leave her thoughts. Those yellow eyes boring into her soul. It gave her the chills again. The hypnotic ability to freeze her in place, as the creature prepared to pounce and kill . . .

Even if they could figure out who it was, how could they fight it? Brittany knew she was powerless to resist its mesmerizing effect, even to save her own life. Sure, they could tell the police, but would they be believed? Brittany could just imagine Sergeant Kahn's response if they suggested to her that it wasn't Kay who was guilty but someone who could turn into a gigantic snake!

Hello, padded cell.

Eventually, though, the day ended. Gathering her books, Brittany slid them into her backpack and silently slipped out of her classroom.

In the hallway, a crooked grin on his face, stood Chad. Despite her fears, Brittany was really glad to see him. After a quick kiss, he gave her a wink. "I've figured it out," he said smugly as Kay hurried over to join them. "Congratulations are in order. Curran has redeemed himself after yesterday's blunders."

"You know who it is?" Brittany asked, hardly able to believe it.

"Tell us! Tell us!" screeched Kay.

"Whoa!" exclaimed Chad. "No, I don't know who it is." Brittany's heart sank. "But," he added, "I *do* know how to find the killer, which is just as good."

"So, how?" growled Kay.

"We need to do DNA testing."

"What?" Kay asked blankly.

"DNA testing," Chad explained. "You know, the

stuff they do in rape cases and in those paternity suits. Everyone's DNA is different, so it's supposed to be an infallible way of fingering culprits."

"Great," said Brittany sourly. "All we have to do is take a skin or blood sample from that snake."

Chad grinned and shook his head. "Or *saliva*," he said. "That's just as distinctive."

"Wonderful," growled Kay. "So one of us has to volunteer to be drooled on by a snake? I know who I'd nominate."

"No!" exclaimed Brittany, catching on to Chad's line of thought. "The *venom!* That would have DNA traces in it!"

"Smart girl," Chad approved. "Right. And your mom has a nice fresh sample sitting in her lab. We can talk her into getting the testing done, I'm sure. Once they find the human DNA in it, then even Kahn is bound to listen to us. All they'll need to do is a DNA test of all the suspects."

"It sounds so simple," Brittany agreed. "I can't help feeling it's not going to be that easy."

"We won't know unless we try," said Kay, her bleak mood lifting. "Chad, I could kiss you." She glanced hastily at Brittany. "A *very* chaste kiss," she added. She gave him a quick peck on the cheek. "You two deserve each other. You're both too brilliant for your own good. So—what are we waiting for? Let's go nail a killer!"

CHAPTER

17

Brittany wasn't surprised that her mother wasn't home when they pulled up. She was most likely still working, even though this was an early closing day at the zoo. When she checked the answering machine, she found two messages. One was a callback from someone her mother had tried to reach. The other was from her mother.

"Hi, Brittany. Just letting you know I'll be late tonight. I've got to finish a couple more tests for Dr. Vitelli and don't know when I'll be done. Bye."

"Great," said Chad. "That means she's got the samples we'd need."

"Yeah." Brittany called her mother's direct line at the zoo. After a few rings, she was frowning. "That's odd. Nobody's picking up." She let it ring another ten times, then hung up. "Why doesn't she answer?"

Kay shrugged. "Maybe she stepped out for a minute."

"I guess," Brittany agreed. "Let's try again in ten minutes." It seemed to take forever for the minutes to pass, then Brittany tried again. There was still no response. "Even if Mom went out," she said, "someone should be there. I'm getting worried." A sudden thought struck her. "You don't think the killer might go for Mom, do you?" Panic started to fill her.

"It's us the snake's after," Chad said firmly. "Why would it go for your mother?"

"To stop her doing the venom tests?" suggested Brittany, her mind a whirl.

"Or as a trap," offered Kay. "A way to get us out to the zoo."

Brittany's heart sank. It made sense.

Chad said, "Let's not panic until there's something to panic about. Maybe your mom had an errand to run. Why don't we go to the zoo and check? If we stick together, we should be able to watch out for each other."

"Good idea," Kay agreed. "I'll just call my folks and let them know."

Chad gave Brittany a hug as Kay made her call.

"Don't worry," he consoled her. "It's probably just a lot of agonizing over nothing. You'll see."

Brittany wished she could believe him. "After these past few days," she replied, "I'm willing to think *anything* could have happened. Even that she's been abducted by Martians."

By the time they pulled into the zoo parking lot, the sun was starting to set. Normally it was a really lovely time of the day here, with the rosy glow behind the tall trees. But the parking lot was virtually empty, and there would be only a skeleton staff on duty—security workers mostly and a few cleaning people.

One of the few cars in the lot was Dr. Harlow's Eagle Talon.

"She's still here," Brittany said anxiously.

"Yeah, but it doesn't prove she's in trouble," Chad reminded her.

"I know." Brittany dashed for the main gate. Naturally it was locked, but she hammered at the booth door until a security guard appeared. Thankfully, it was one whom she recognized. "Hi, Bill!" she called. "It's me—Brittany. I'm kind of worried about my mom."

Bill opened the door, frowning as he saw their anxious faces. He was a tall, stocky man in his fifties with a sympathetic smile. "She's still here, Brittany," he replied. "Over in her lab, I assume."

"She's not answering the phone," Brittany told him. "Is it okay for us to go over there?"

"I guess. But stick to the paths, okay?" He hefted

his walkie-talkie. "I'll have one of my men stop by there. Better safe and all that."

"Thanks." She started down the familiar pathways. The low-level lighting around the park was starting to flicker on, and a couple of stars were barely visible. Brittany's heart was thumping as she ran, and not simply because of the exertion. *Be all right!* she willed. *Please be all right!*

They could see lights on in her mother's lab as they reached the door, panting for breath. Brittany steeled herself for whatever she might find, and then threw open the door. She tumbled into the laboratory, Kay and Chad close behind her.

Dr. Harlow looked up in surprise from her microscope at the other end of the lab. "Brittany!" she exclaimed. "What on earth are you doing here?"

"Mom!" Brittany yelled. "You're okay!" She felt a great weight lift.

"Of course I am," her mother answered. "Why shouldn't I be?"

"You didn't answer the phone," Chad said.

Dr. Harlow glanced down at it. "Oh. Was that you calling? I'm afraid I was in the middle of testing this venom sample, and I didn't want to be distracted."

Relieved that all her worries and fears had been for nothing, Brittany almost collapsed onto a stool. "You gave us such a scare!" she told her mother.

"I can't think why." Her mom shook her head, smiling fondly at her daughter. "Honest, I'm old enough to stay out after dark."

Chad stepped forward. "Yeah, I guess we just went

overboard a bit," he admitted. He looked at the microscope. "Is that the venom sample from Curtis's blood?"

The door opened, and one of the security men stuck his head in. "Hi, Doc!" he called. "Everything okay?"

"Fine, Alec," she replied vaguely. "Just my daughter worrying too much."

"Okay." He disappeared, and the door closed again. Brittany heard the crackle of his radio as he made his report.

"Is that the venom?" repeated Chad.

"Oh, yes, that's it." Dr. Harlow tapped the microscope. "I've just got a few more tests to do, but there's no doubt in my mind that it's the same poison that killed that Witney boy."

"The same concentration?" Kay asked. "I mean, enough to kill a herd of elephants?"

"Yes, actually," admitted Brittany's mother. "Virtually an identical dose. Curious, isn't it?"

"Speaking of curious," Chad said, "is it possible to run a DNA test on that venom?"

Dr. Harlow asked, "What on earth for?"

"To find out who killed Curtis," said Kay.

"But . . ." Brittany's mother looked as if she didn't know whether to laugh or scream. "It won't tell you anything. It *can't*. There must be the venom of a dozen or more snakes here, all mixed together."

"I don't think so," Brittany told her mother. "It's just one snake. We've seen it."

"You have?" Her mother was definitely losing the threads of this conversation. "When? How?"

"Last night," Brittany replied. "It attacked us." She told her mother the entire story then because she hadn't seen her earlier. Dr. Harlow sat on her stool, confused. "So you see," Brittany finished, "since it's just one snake and since it *must* be some kind of shape-shifter, if we can run a DNA analysis, that should give us the killer's DNA pattern. Then we just take samples from all the suspects and match them."

"Bingo," said Chad. "We nail the killer." He smiled modestly. "It was all my idea. What do you think?"

"I think you've all gone stark, staring mad," Dr. Harlow said. "I've never heard such a pack of foolishness in my life! Giant snakes indeed! Honestly, Brittany, couldn't you think of anything more believable than that to try to fool me with?"

Brittany couldn't believe the scorn in her mother's voice. "Mom," she gasped brokenly, "it's the *truth*. We *did* see an impossibly huge snake. And it *has* to be someone who can do what that book suggests."

"What book?"

Brittany pulled it from her bag and showed it to her mother. Dr. Harlow laughed and shook her head. "Honestly, Brit, you do fill your head with some nonsense. That's not a serious work. Vande Water is a little . . ." She made a circular gesture with her finger next to her temple. "He writes about all kinds of weird subjects. I don't think even he believes half of it."

"Well, *I* do!" Kay yelled with a ferocity that shook even Brittany. "Stop being so scientific and rational for a second, will you? Listen to Brittany. Has she ever lied to you? Or tried to trick you?"

Dr. Harlow was taken aback. "Well, no—" she began.

"Then at least *try* to hear what she's saying," Kay continued fiercely. "Maybe you don't believe it, but we do. Isn't that enough for you to just run one more test on that sample?"

"Kay, that's enough," Brittany said quietly. "Please don't harass my mom."

"No, it's okay," her mother said. "She's right. I'm sorry, all of you. Thank you, Kay. Of course I should at least try to prove that you're wrong, rather than just *saying* it. And I'd like to, but I don't have the equipment."

Brittany's heart sank again. After all their bright ideas, to be stopped like this!

Dr. Harlow smiled slightly. "But Dr. Vitelli does," she added. "If I can get a reasonably pure sample of the venom, uncontaminated by Curtis's blood, then *he* could do the test."

"Way to go!" Chad cried.

"Thanks, Mom," said Brittany happily. "You won't regret it, I promise."

Her mother shook her head. "Not if it makes you happy, I won't. But it's just a waste of time. I can tell you now that nothing will come of this."

"We'll take that chance," Kay told her.

"Okay." Dr. Harlow stood up. "While I start the purification, would you mind fetching Christina?" she asked her daughter. "She's a whiz with that equipment."

"No problem," agreed Brittany. "Where is she?"

"Over in the Midnight World," her mother answered. "Checking on the vipers for me. They seem awfully broody lately." She looked at Chad and Kay. "And I'd appreciate it if the two of you went with her, rather than harassing me."

"No sweat," Chad agreed. "I aim to keep your daughter in my sight at all times."

"And I'll be chaperon," added Kay, grinning wickedly. "It wouldn't do for them to get frisky in all that darkness inside the Midnight World."

Dr. Harlow laughed. "I'll call Dr. Vitelli and set up the tests while you're gone."

Feeling much better, Brittany led the way to the Midnight World building. They could be on their way to getting some kind of a solution now! Chad was bound to get a promotion and maybe even one of those literary awards he wanted so badly.

It was continuing to get dark. Without the lights the zoo would be only shadows and shapes. Brittany could hear the animals call out as they started to settle down for the night. As the three of them entered the Midnight World, they stepped from darkness to bright light.

"Whoa!" said Chad. "I should have brought my shades! This doesn't look much like midnight to me!"

"Of course not," Brittany told him, laughing. "That's during the *day*. At night, the lights come on. The animals can go to sleep then and wake up to the darkness in here in the morning."

"I wouldn't have thought even bats could sleep in this light," grumbled Chad.

"You'd be surprised," Brittany told him. She glanced around and saw that a door marked Employees Only was slightly ajar. "Christina must be in there. Come on." She pushed the door open and called out the assistant's name.

"Back here, Brittany!" came the cheery reply from deeper inside.

Brittany led the way through the maze of supply racks and cleaning equipment. "We're behind the exhibits back here," she explained. To their right ran a low wall, surmounted by huge glass windows. Doors in this wall led to the various tanks and runs that fronted on the public area. She spotted Christina and waved.

The assistant came out into the corridor, carefully closing and locking the door behind her. "Hi, Brit," she said. "What's up?"

"Mom needs a hand back at the lab," she told the young woman. "She claims you're the tops with the purifier."

Christina laughed. "Like I always say, I love working with your mother. It's kind of her to say so."

"How are the vipers?" Chad asked. "Dr. Harlow said they might be having troubles."

"I think she just worries too much," Christina said. "They're all fine." They came to the door to the public area, and Christina let them out before closing it firmly. Glancing across the room, she nodded to another of the exhibits. "Which is more than you can say for the fennecs."

Brittany moved over to get a better look at her

favorite animals. Both of the foxes looked as if they were throwing temper tantrums. Their large ears were raised, their fur bristling, and their teeth bared. Even through the thick glass, she could hear their snarls.

"Weird little things," muttered Kay. "Not very friendly, are they?"

Icy tendrils wrapped themselves around Brittany's spine. She'd seen this kind of thing before. Slowly she turned to stare at Christina. "It's *you* they're afraid of," she gasped. "Isn't it? *You're* the snake being. You're the lamia!"

CHAPTER

18

Christina gave a brittle laugh and a blank stare. "What *are* you talking about?" she asked.

"It's you," Brittany repeated. She gestured at the fennecs, who were still hissing and spitting. "I saw cats behave that way at the cat show. They went crazy like that over Curtis. I guess it was because he'd been bitten by the snake."

"Right," agreed Chad. "They acted *exactly* like those foxes. There are just four of us here, and we know *we're* not snakes. So you *must* be."

Christina shook her head. "You're crazy! There's no such thing as a lamia! That's just a legend. Women turning into snakes!"

"It's no good," Brittany told her. "We *know* it's you."

"You've got to be joking!" Christina insisted. "You can't possibly believe what you're saying."

"It's you," hissed Kay with utter certainty. "You killed Grant, and Jeff, and Curtis. And you tried to kill us last night!" Her anger had been building, and it finally exploded. "And I'll prove it!" She leaped forward and struck with her hand. Fingers open, she raked thick welts down Christina's cheek.

The assistant cried out and staggered back, clutching her bleeding cheek. Bright blood bubbled from the cuts. Christina screamed—half pain, half fury. But Kay wasn't finished with her. She grabbed Christina's wrist and slowly forced the hand away from the cheek.

It was incredible. Brittany gave a gasp as she watched.

The cuts were closing up as she stared at them. The blood had dripped down Christina's cheek onto her blouse. In its wake, fresh skin had formed. In seconds nothing was left of the wounds but the stains on Christina's blouse.

"Tell us we imagined *that!*" snapped Kay.

Christina took a deep breath, ready to start her denials again. But their expressions must have convinced her it was futile. She snarled and succeeded in jerking her hand free from Kay's grip and backed up to the wall beside the fennecs. The two foxes were almost frothing at the mouth in their futile attempts to claw through the glass and attack her. Her head whipped around, and she glared furiously at the animals. "Be still!" she hissed.

The two creatures acted as if they'd been struck by a brick. Both collapsed soundlessly.

Brittany started to move forward, but Christina jerked around again, glowering at the three of them. All of her charm and poise had fallen from her now. She braced herself against the wall, her mouth twisted in a snarl, her eyes filled with hatred.

"All right," she whispered. "I admit it. I *am* the lamia, the snake woman. But you'll never prove it."

"Yes, we will," Brittany told her coldly. "You have the same steroids in your blood that Curtis and Grant had. You must get them from the same source. All the police have to do is to tie you to them through that, and you're finished."

"You fool!" snarled Christina. "Source? I *am* the source!"

"What are you talking about?" Kay asked, shaken and puzzled.

"The steroids are not a drug," Christina told them. "It's what I am. It's in my blood. I gave of myself to Grant and Curtis. I regenerated them, and my blood regenerates me."

"Then that should be even simpler to prove," Chad said. "Dr. Harlow is getting the venom tested in a DNA sampler. I'm willing to bet that it will show human DNA—and that it will match that from those bloodstains on your clothing perfectly."

Christina stared at them, anger and disbelief warring for control of her emotions. Her anger won. "You *fools!*" she hissed. "Do you think I would allow that?"

Sudden fear struck Brittany. She had almost forgotten the power of the snake inside the small young woman. Now she realized what Christina meant.

But it was too late.

Freezing coldness passed into her body, striking through to the marrow of her bones. The chill froze her in place as nausea flashed through her. Terror filled every cell in her body.

Christina's eyes changed as Brittany stared fixedly at her. A sickly yellow seemed to wash out the pale blue of her eyes. Then Christina's eyes were no more, replaced by the slitted yellow eyes of a snake. Unable to move a muscle, Brittany could only watch in helpless fear and fascination.

The beautiful, angular face seemed to shiver as she watched, and the short-cropped hair began to melt into olive-green scales. The pert nose flattened and became two gashes in skin that became darker by the second. The pink tongue darkened and lengthened, the end forking and flickering.

Two long, curved fangs slowly sprouted from the roof of her mouth.

Then the change halted. Christina was caught midway between woman and serpent. She had a serpent's head, but still had her female form, though her skin was leathery and scaly. Hissing, her mouth slowly broadened into a feral smile.

"Now," she almost purred, "tell me what you can do!"

Brittany struggled, but it was no use. She was frozen in place, her skin ice-cold. She would freak out, except she couldn't even . . .

She *could* speak!

Unlike the previous times, Brittany did have some small control over her head. She could gasp out words, and she could move her eyes slightly to focus on Christina. The sight of the half-snake woman was sickening; the thought of what she was even worse. "What are you?" she gasped.

"What?" Christina smiled again, and her forked tongue flickered in the air. "But you already guessed that. I'm a lamia—a snake-woman, if you like."

"How?" Chad managed to ask.

"How is it possible, you mean?" Christina laughed—a harsh, unpleasant sound. "Always the reporter, aren't you? Want an interview with the lamia, perhaps?" She considered the idea for a moment, then let out her breath in a low, soft hiss. "Well, why not?" Her features softened a little, and her face became slightly more human. If anything, Brittany thought, being able to see parts of Christina in the snake face made the effect even more repulsive.

Then Christina turned to look at Brittany. "You shouldn't have done this, you know. I *do* like you, and your handsome little boyfriend." Her eyes darted to Kay. "Not you, though," she admitted.

"You tried to kill me," gasped Brittany.

John Peel

Christina shrugged. "It was the blood-lust, I'm afraid. I couldn't help it. Sometimes a mood just overtakes me, and I have no choice but to hunt and kill. . . ." She shivered at the thought. "And you *are* a threat to me. I imagine that you plan to expose me and have me arrested?" She sighed. "Don't bother to deny it. I can tell. A lot of people feel that way at first. Like that stupid reporter who tracked me down. He remembered a similar mysterious death in the last town I lived in. But . . ." She licked her lips and studied the three of them. "There is another option. Let me explain about myself so you'll understand."

Slowly she started to pace up and down in front of them. A thrill of horror swept through Brittany. Christina was like a snake playing with its helpless prey before it strikes.

"I was born in Greece," Christina explained, "about three thousand years ago."

"Three thousand?" whispered Chad.

"Yes." Christina smiled. "I don't look my age, do I? I was born into a noble family there and was given over to become a priestess of Apollo, to train at the Oracle of Delphi. You can't imagine what that place was like." She became lost in her memories. "It was a large temple beside a cave, where the Sun God himself was supposed to appear to his priestesses. People would come to the shrine from all over Greece to ask questions of the Oracle or the priestess. She would consult with the god and then utter prophecies that were almost always correct.

"I was not the Oracle, of course, but I hungered to

192

know the truth, and I managed to discover it. The cave was situated in a volcanic region. A crack in the floor of the cave linked it to a volcanic vent. Gases would escape up from this fissure and into the cave. The Oracle had a three-legged stool or tripod constructed over the fissure and would breath in the volcanic gases. Somehow the gases caused her mind to be wrenched free of her body, and in her exalted state, she could see and foretell the future.

"Knowing the secret, I wanted to experience the gift. Greece at that time was politically unstable, but we at the temple were usually left alone. None of the soldiers, no matter how bloodthirsty, would tangle with the handmaidens of a god. Besides, most of them only wanted to hear that they would win their stupid little wars. So mostly we were safe. One warrior, a general, wasn't kind and had looted a couple of the other temples. The Oracle was certain he'd do the same to Delphi, so she ordered us into the hills to hide until his men had passed by.

"I knew that this was my chance. I could never have gotten into the vision chamber normally. It was well guarded and only the Oracle was allowed inside. But when everyone fled for safety, I hid. When I was alone, I entered the sacred chamber and sat on the tripod, above the vent. I knew that this was what I had been born for. The gases swirled about me, and I felt as if my head were about to explode.

"In a trance I saw a snake. The snake was a creature sacred to Apollo, so this was no surprise. But in the vision the god himself appeared. He was tall and muscular, a perfect athlete. He slew the snake and extracted its poison. This he blended with the extracts from certain plants, and then he offered the cup to me.

"'Drink,' he told me. 'And you will become immortal, like me.' And in the vision I drank the potion. Then I awoke to find myself still seated on the tripod. Standing before me, a sword at my throat, was the general.

"He would have killed me had I not told him of my vision. The thought of immortality appealed to him, of course, so he spared my life. I was allowed to make the potion that I had seen. When it was complete, this general planned to drink it. But first, of course, I was to test it. He wanted to see if I lived or died.

"I had no option but to take it. Not that I would have refused. I was utterly convinced then that Apollo had given me this as a gift for my devotion. I drained the potion, and fire consumed my stomach. I fell, screaming, to the floor. The general would have slain me, but he was enjoying the effect that the supposed poison was having on me. I writhed in agony as the liquid filled my body.

"And then I changed. The potion did not kill me. Instead, it blended the nature of the snake with my nature. I was transformed into a gigantic snake. The general was terrified and ran at me with his sword. But I struck first, sinking my fangs into his neck and slaying him. His men, thinking I was a creature of the gods, fled.

"I was terrified that I had turned permanently into a

snake, but I discovered that by concentrating, I could change back into my human form again. Then I gradually discovered everything had been affected inside of me.

"I had become virtually immortal. Others about me aged and withered and died, but I stayed eternally young. In three millennia I have not aged a day. I also discovered that my body had developed an immense capacity for healing. Wounds would heal instantly and I never became sick. I don't think that I'm indestructible, but wounds that would kill a normal human do not kill me. I wandered the world, learning and enjoying life.

"I remember once I had my hand cut off for some reason." She held up her right fist. "It grew back again within weeks. I killed the man who had done it." She shook her head as if throwing off the old memories. "I have changed my name and my identity many, many times before I arrived here. I like it here." She looked at Brittany. "Your mother is good to me, and my work here is interesting and fulfilling. People were, at first, very friendly."

Brittany stared back at Christina in horror. "But what about Grant?"

"Grant!" The snake-woman smiled again, her tongue flickering. "Perhaps because of Apollo I have a soft spot for athletic young men. Especially if they aren't too bright. I think you'll agree that Grant was all of that. One of the things I discovered very early on about myself is that I can alter my venom. It can either be highly lethal or else it can be that steroidlike substance. If I inject it into other people, it transfers some of my health and strength. People become much healthier, and they become much more athletic."

"But the effect doesn't last," Brittany guessed.

"No," Christina admitted. "It's effective for only a few weeks. Then I have to renew the dosage." She laughed, that disgusting, reptilian snicker again. "It kept most of my men firmly in line, of course. If they wanted the venom, they made sure they stayed on my good side. But that never lasts, either. Sooner or later they all turn from me, and I have to kill them."

She glared at Kay. "You took Grant away from me before I had tired of him. I don't ask much from my consorts, but I do demand their loyalty and undivided attention. Grant was incapable of giving me that, it seems." She smirked. "He couldn't give it to you, either. I had no choice but to kill him."

"And Curtis?" asked Brittany.

"That was a mistake," admitted Christina. "I was in a hurry. He was hungry for my elixir. I should have waited until the fuss over Grant died down, but I made a stupid error. I realized almost immediately that Curtis was the wrong person for me. He was too scared, too nervous, and unstable. I had to kill him before he broke down and told you all that he knew."

"And Jeff Chaney?" Chad said.

Christina shrugged. "He was getting annoying. I could have avoided him, but the blood-lust was on me and it was so much more satisfying just to kill him and be done with it."

"You tried to kill me, too," Brittany gasped.

"Yes," admitted Christina. She seemed to be calming down, as if she'd reached some decision. "When I killed Grant, I knew that you had sensed me. I believed that you had heard me arguing with him in the locker room before I killed him. I felt that I had no option but to kill you. However, I am prepared to offer you another path."

"Which is?"

"Join me," Christina said simply. "Give me your word not to expose me, and I will give you the gift of life and healing." She stood in front of Brittany. "It will even heal your eyes, so that you don't have to wear glasses."

The thought of having her sight healed was thrilling, but Brittany hated the rest of it. "What about Chad and Kay?" she asked, playing along.

Christina looked at the other two. "Chad—well, I'm sure we could find some use for him. I'll include him if he agrees to keep our secret. As for Kay . . ." She shook her head. "I have another use for her. The police need a murderer, and that delightfully dull Sergeant Kahn has decided that Kay is the killer. So I aim to provide the police with a dead suspect. They will feel that they have their killer and I will go free. Especially if you and Chad back up my story that Kay went crazy and tried to kill me next, but died by her own lethal weapon."

Kill Kay? Brittany was sick even thinking about it. "No deal," she gasped. "I won't let you kill my friend."

"Don't be stupid!" Christina cried. "I'm going to kill her anyway. So why should you die as well?"

Brittany wished she could shake her head or spit at Christina, but all she could do was say, "I won't help you. Not at that cost."

"Thanks, Brit," Kay whispered.

"Idiot!" Christina yelled. Then she turned to Chad. "And what about you?" she asked, seductively. "You're a little brighter than most men I go for, but you look good. Join me and I'll make you stronger and better."

Chad made an odd, barking noise. Brittany realized it was all the laughter he could produce. "And trust you? Like Curtis and Grant did? So that when you don't like me, or don't trust me, or just get bored, it'll be the venom instead of life you give me? Forget it. If you kill Brittany, you'll have to kill me, too. Or I promise that I'll kill you."

Brittany was thrilled that he preferred to die with her than to live with Christina. If she hadn't been paralyzed, she would have run to him and hugged him tight. But all she could do was gasp, "I love you, Chad."

"I love you, too, Brit," he replied. "It's a shame we can't do anything about it, isn't it?"

Christina whirled around in fury. "You stupid imbeciles!" she screamed. "I'll make you pay for this!

I'll make you all pay for it! Even if I have to vanish and start a new life over again. The three of you are dead!" She faced Chad. "Starting with you." She gave Brittany a malevolent smile. "I'll let you watch me kill your friends, first, and then it will be your turn." Hissing with anger and blood-lust, she opened her mouth. The two poison fangs were down and dripping venom as she moved slowly toward Chad.

CHAPTER

19

If Brittany had been terrified before, there was no one word to describe her feelings now. Panic, and disgust, and fear waged war inside her with hatred for Christina and despair at the thought of seeing Chad murdered.

She had lost one person whom she loved, whom she'd been unable to help. Her father had died, far away, falling in flames from the sky. That loss had been agonizing. Watching Christina murder Chad would be too much to bear.

"No!" she gasped. "I won't let you do it! You *won't* kill him!"

The lamia simply laughed that sibilant hiss of hers and ignored the futile threat. She drew back her head, ready to fasten her fangs into Chad's immobile throat.

"No!" screamed Brittany, her terror building inside her to an unbearable pitch. A veil of red blotted out her mind. She couldn't lose Chad! She *couldn't!* Without even being aware of it, she snapped through the paralyzing chains that held her and staggered forward.

Christina heard the movement and whirled around. Her slitted eyes widened as she saw that Brittany had broken free. Brittany's feelings, fears, and frustrations all centered on one person. With a wordless scream of rage, she swung her fist. It slammed hard into the snake-thing's stomach. The jolt of pain from the blow shuddered through Brittany's arm and body and broke the mindless rage for a moment.

Howling and gasping for breath, Christina flew back across the room. Brittany could see the pain on her features, and also the shock and bewilderment. She was clearly not used to anyone breaking free of her control. It sapped at her certainty and strength. As Brittany watched, Chad moved his fingers and then his arm.

"It's not possible!" gasped Christina, huddled over, clutching her stomach. "You *can't* resist me! No one can!"

Brittany crouched, watching the lamia. "You *won't*

kill him!" she snarled back. "I won't let you! I won't lose him!"

Kay, too, was managing to break the paralyzing hold, and as each second passed, Christina was losing her confidence. She had never been faced down before.

"You're finished," Brittany spat. "You can't fight us—not when we can move. You'll never kill us now!"

This sank in to Christina—in a matter of seconds she would be facing three of them, all furious and determined.

She spun around, her skin rippling and quivering. With an incoherent cry she darted for the door, half slithering as she moved.

Brittany wanted to go after her, to stop her. But she knew that alone she would stand no chance. She had to stay with Chad and Kay so the three of them could take on the snake-woman. She gripped Chad. "Come on!" she encouraged him. "Shake it off! You can do it!"

She could see the sweat on his forehead and the effort he was putting into fighting off the freeze in his limbs. His hands and legs shook before he managed to stagger forward a step.

"Atta gal," he managed to gasp. "I'm proud of you, Brit. You beat her!" Then he grabbed her arms with unsteady hands. "And you saved my life."

"Get grateful later," she told him. "We've got to find her before she gets away." She turned to Kay, who stood shaking with her arms wrapped tight around herself. She seemed to be in a state of shock, but her eyes opened when Brittany called her name.

"I'm ready," she said softly. "Thank you, Brit." Then she moved toward the door to the service area and opened it. "Come on, guys."

"Uh, she went the other way," Chad commented.

"Right," Kay agreed. "You going to get her with your bare hands?" She threw out a broom. "We need something to fight her with."

Understanding lit Chad's face. "Right!" He whacked the broom hard on the floor, sending the head flying and leaving himself with a long pole. "Let's go snake thrashing."

Brittany wished she'd thought of the idea. Grabbing a mop, she smacked the head off it. Kay was already armed. Together, each holding a weapon, they moved out the door.

It was completely dark outside now. Only pale circles of light around the lamps stood out on the ground. Brittany had always liked the shade cast by the many trees, but now it simply meant there were more places for Christina to hide. Overhead, there was no moon. Thousands of stars were scattered across the sky, but they provided next to no light to help their search.

"Which way?" Chad asked, peering about uncertainly.

What would Christina do next? Brittany tried to imagine. A terrible thought came to her. "My mom," she whispered. Scared that Christina would be out for blood and revenge, she started to sprint back toward her mother's lab. She heard both Kay and Chad falling in behind her. As she ran, she felt fear rising inside her. Was she right? Or was she letting her fear overcome her reasoning?

Suddenly she halted. Chad and Kay only just avoided running into her. Before they could ask questions, she held up her free hand. "Listen!"

Over a few cries in the night, one sound was impossible to miss. Brittany could hear the deep, bellowing roar of an enraged elephant. It was screaming and trumpeting. These cries were accompanied by a faint crashing sound.

"The elephants!" she cried. "They sound like they're throwing a fit!"

"Christina!" said Chad. "It's a dead giveaway."

They whirled around and ran toward the elephant compound. As they ran, Kay called out, "She's not as smart as she thinks. Taking a job in a zoo when she has this effect on animals!"

"All animals," Brittany gasped. "Except reptiles."

"Feels at home here!" Chad was almost laughing at the thought.

"She'll be locked up all right," Brittany agreed.

Panting, they drew closer to the screaming pachyderms. They all slowed down, worried about an ambush. Brittany, chest heaving, lifted her broomstick. "Can you see her?"

Chad peered through the gloom. In the pit below, the elephants were bucking, rearing, and screaming out their fear and anger. "No," he said. "Nothing but mad elephants."

"There!" exclaimed Kay, using her pole to point.

In the shadows off to the left there was a huddled shape. In the dim light Brittany couldn't make out much but the blouse that Christina was wearing. It was a light color. There was no movement at all.

"Careful," Chad said, taking the lead as they made a dash for the shape. Brittany and Kay were only a pace behind him, their weapons raised. Astonishingly, Christina didn't try to escape.

"Oh, God!" said Chad, staring down at the bundle. Brittany couldn't get her voice to work. She was too afraid that she was about to throw up. What they were looking down at was too gross, too unbelievable.

It was Christina's clothing, draped about Christina's skin. There was no mistaking that face and the short blond hair. But it wasn't Christina. A long gash down the face and the exposed portions of the flesh made that clear. Somehow, like a snake, Christina had shed her skin. Ripped out of it from the inside, leaving it behind her.

Brittany tore her eyes away from it, not wanting to see any more details. "She's . . . changing," she whispered. "That's her old skin. She's growing a new one."

"It's disgusting," Kay murmured, clearly on the verge of barfing at what they had seen.

"We've got to find her!" Chad snapped. Brittany could see the struggle he was undergoing to keep from throwing up as well. "She might be able to change her features, to look like someone else! If we don't find her—"

"Freeze!"

Despite the cry, they all whirled around, shocked. Brittany found herself staring at the business end of two guns. Behind one stood Sergeant Kahn; behind the second her portly partner, Jellicoe. He was panting from the running he'd been doing, but Kahn was as composed as ever.

"I knew tagging around you would pay off, Johnson," she said triumphantly. "But I didn't think I'd find you with another body." She glanced at Brittany and Chad. "Or partners in crime."

"You're wrong!" Brittany exclaimed. How could this be happening? It couldn't have come at a worse time. "This isn't a body!"

"Sure looks like one to me," Kahn answered, the revolver in her hand panning to cover each of them in turn.

"You need to take a closer look, Sergeant," Chad suggested. "We'll step back. Then examine it."

Kahn's eyes narrowed in suspicion. "All right. Move away. But remember you're covered." As the three of them moved back, the woman stepped forward cautiously. Only when she was right beside the "body" did she look down at it. "What the hell?" Her thin face went deathly pale.

"It's Christina's skin," Kay told her. "Not her corpse. She's the killer. We almost had her! If you weren't so certain it was me, we could have nailed her!"

"We still can," Chad snapped. "Listen!"

Brittany pricked up her ears, but even over the elephantine groans, the roaring and screaming of the lions was more than apparent. "It's got to be her!" she cried. She stared at the shaken Kahn. "Believe us!" she begged. "It's Christina! She's your killer. But we've got to stop her!"

Kahn shook her head slowly, fighting back the horrors facing her. "But it's not possible!"

"Forget possible," Kay snarled. "It's *her*. And I'm going to get her." She glared at the detective. "The only way to stop me is to shoot me. And I'll either sue you or haunt you if you do!" She spun about and started off in the direction of the lions' cries.

Jellicoe raised his gun, and Brittany was certain for one sick moment that he was going to shoot Kay in the back. But he didn't. He and Kahn took off after her. "Come on," she snapped.

It was really freaky to be running after Kay down dark pathways. Brittany hoped they would be in time. The two police officers ran with her and Chad, though it was clear that neither understood anything that was going on.

Then they were in the open plaza beside the lion den. There was a closed souvenir booth, several trash baskets, and a few benches. Around the den itself was a fence, then shrubs. Beyond that was a drop, and then the den itself. From all the roaring and screaming, both the lion and the two lionesses that shared it with him were up and frantic. They roared and spat and screamed into the night.

Kay was searching for any sign of Christina as they arrived. "Split up," she called without turning. "She's got to be here somewhere."

"But . . ." Kahn began. Then she swallowed. "That was her *skin?*"

"Yeah," Brittany answered.

"Then . . . *what* are we looking for?"

Brittany shrugged. "Maybe a giant snake. Maybe a naked person. We don't know. But it'll be *her*. And she's very, very deadly, so watch out." To her surprise, the sergeant nodded her understanding. Kahn maybe wasn't the dumb cop that Brittany had assumed her to be. The police officer gestured with her free hand for Jellicoe to move left, covering Chad. She herself stuck fairly close to Brittany, her eyes skimming the gloom, the muzzle of her gun following her every move.

"I'm not sure I believe this," she muttered. "Any of it. A *snake?*"

"Just look," suggested Brittany. "I'll explain everything later."

Hunting in the shadows for—what?—was draining all of Brittany's remaining strength and courage. She swallowed, but her throat was dry. She could hear the hammering of her heart, and she was breathing in short gasps. Some of that was because of the exertion, but most of it was simple fear. She needed to find a bathroom very badly, but it would have to wait.

There was a sudden explosion of movement from the bushes to the left. Jellicoe gave a yelp as *something* was on him. There was the bark of his gun and a horrible cry.

Brittany whipped around, her pole raised and tightly clenched in both hands. Christina was on top of Jellicoe, her fangs buried in his neck.

At least, it *had* to be Christina. This was the most horrific transformation of them all. In the eerie light of the lamps she seemed to glow. She was naked, and much worse. Her skin glistened and was transparent —just like a snake's when it emerges from its old skin. Every vein, every muscle, was visible through the glasslike skin. The thing was devoid of hair.

It took all of Brittany's courage to stand still and stare.

Christina's head came up. The skin there was just as wet and invisible. Veins lined the ugly face, and the tongue flicked out between the fangs. The yellow eyeballs were huge with no lids to cover them. Even at a distance, the throbbing of the veins in Christina's temples was clear.

"God," whispered Kahn in shock. But she pulled up her hand and fired.

The bullet slammed into the thing's shoulder. Christina screamed, tumbling back off the rigid, dead body of Jellicoe. Then the disgusting creature staggered to its feet. The ruptured hole in Christina's shoulder was already starting to crawl closed, and its blood was seeping instead of gushing.

Chad moved like lightning, whipping his pole around so fast that he would have made a movie Robin Hood wielding a quarterstaff look slow. The blow caught Christina below the ribs, and sent her staggering back toward the fence.

All vestiges of her humanity shed by now, Christina didn't scream or talk. She was reacting merely as an animal. Panting and limping, she managed to regain her feet as Kahn fired a second time.

The bullet cut a red groove down the fleeing thing's side. Immediately, though, the wound started to close up.

"She heals too fast!" Brittany screamed as she ran beside Kahn. "This is no good!"

"Then how do we stop her? It?"

"I was hoping you had an idea." She shut up so she could concentrate on running.

Christina was beside the fence now, rushing toward an exit. With every step she grew stronger. Kay caught up with her first and slid the tip of her broom handle between Christina's legs. With a cry of pain and rage the thing went flying.

The snake-thing landed, then rose to its feet again. Brittany heard Christina hissing out in fury and agony. She saw the glint of the yellow eyes and the glistening, see-through skin. Then the creature scaled the fence, to leap over. It must have forgotten what lay beyond the fence in its panic.

Kahn fired again. This time the bullet caught Christina in the chest. Even as the wound spurted blood, it began to heal.

The force of the blow threw the transparent thing off its shaky perch on the fence. Christina fell backward with a howl.

The four of them dashed to the fence and heard the

lions move into action. Next came a terrible scream from Christina.

The three giant cats must have been as terrified as they were angry. Snarling, they reached the snake-thing as it struggled to its feet. It opened its mouth to hiss, but its power to paralyze had faded. She was running out of endurance.

Brittany shuddered and turned away as the lions sprang. There was the sound of snapping jaws. Christina's cry cut off and there was the distinct crunch of a bone being crushed.

Even Kahn turned away. The hand holding her gun lowered, shaking. The lions continued to tear and slash.

Kay turned to Brittany. "Want to bet she doesn't recover from those wounds?" she whispered.

EPILOGUE

Brittany was glad that Chad had his arm around her. She was sure that if he wasn't holding on to her she'd faint. And, after everything she'd endured that night, that would be humiliating. Besides, it felt good having him hold her.

All three of them were in her mother's lab. Mom had made them all steaming mugs of instant coffee and had thankfully asked no questions in the half-hour since they had arrived, shaking and exhausted. She had simply sat there and held Brittany's hand.

The door opened and Sergeant Kahn walked in, paler than normal and looking exhausted. Determination kept her moving.

"I'm very grateful for your help," she told them. "Now listen up. I'm going to tell you what happened."

"But—" Kay began.

"Listen, I said!" Kahn glared at her. "We all agree that Christina was the killer, but there was no snake, understand?"

"What?" asked Brittany, shaken.

"Nobody will believe it," the officer said simply. "Hell, *I* don't believe what I saw. As far as anyone else is concerned, she was just a crazy woman who killed Witney, Harlow, Chaney, and Al Jellicoe. I shot her and she fell into the lion pit. End of story. Understand?"

"But what about her skin?" Brittany asked, her own crawling as she remembered it.

"I threw that in after her," Kahn said grimly. "The lions tore it to bits along with the rest of her. Everyone will think it was on her. Let them think it."

Kay managed to nod. "I guess you're right," she agreed. "It sounds better your way, doesn't it?"

"Damned straight," the sergeant agreed. Then she rested a hand on Kay's shoulder. "For what it's worth, I'm sorry."

Kay smiled. It was thin and uncertain, but it was a smile.

Kahn nodded and gave them all one last look. "Right. So don't forget our story. 'Cause if any of you tries telling the truth, I'm not going to back you up." Then she managed a wink. "Thanks, guys."

Watching her go, Brittany snuggled up next to Chad. "Well," she said. "Now what?"

Chad looked down at her. "Well, there are a few things I have to check up on," he said.

"Damn your story," she muttered, irritated that he had to go to work.

"My thoughts exactly," he agreed. "I was thinking about how you saved my life. And said you loved me." He bent his head and kissed her, right in front of her mother and Kay. Brittany wasn't at all embarrassed and instantly began to feel better.

Maybe there was hope that the rest of the world would, too.

"Oh, gross," said Kay. "If there's one thing I *really* can't stand, it's someone else getting the guy and the happy ending."

About the Author

JOHN PEEL was born in Nottingham, England, the oldest of seven children, and he attended Nottingham University. He moved to the United States to marry his pen pal, Nan. They live in Manorville, New York, with their wire-haired fox terrier, Dashiell, who frequently wants John to stop writing to play ball.

John is the author of numerous science-fiction and mystery novels for young adults, and he has been a contributing editor and writer for several magazines. His novels *Talons, Shattered,* and *Poison* are available from Archway Paperbacks, and *Prisoners of Peace,* a *Star Trek: Deep Space Nine*® title, is available from Minstrel Books. His next young-adult thriller from Archway Paperbacks is *Maniac,* coming in June 1994.

ENTER INTO THE WORLD OF MAGIC AND MADNESS

with

JOHN PEEL

→ TALONS ←

It plummeted from the sky at midnight, a huge, winged predator, talons unfurled, on a mission of death....

→ SHATTERED ←

The scarab of death is coming to steal her soul!

And Don't Miss...

→ POISON ←

Something evil this way comes... Death by Venom!

Available from Archway Paperbacks
Published by Pocket Books

864-02